"You Only Have To Donate Your Body," Jan Said.

"We're auctioning off men as dates for women bidders."

"No."

Realizing she had taken a belligerent stance, she modified it, crossing her arms over her chest. But that was just as bad, and finally she let her arms hang loose. Her tone was reasonable. "You'd be in good company. And it's for a good cause."

He didn't reply, but he didn't leave, either. So she said, "Please. We need one more man to volunteer for the auction."

"Are you going to bid?" Junior asked.

She was businesslike but gentle. "The committee members will put in base bids on each man. But lots of women will be competing. You'll be a prime draw. You're very nice looking and . . . well made."

"I can also walk and talk."

She retorted primly, "I really wouldn't know about that. I haven't seen much of you lately."

"No, you haven't. But then you never could."

Dear Reader:

Happy New Year! 1991 is going to be a terrific year at Silhouette Desire. We've got some wonderful things planned, starting with another of those enticing, irresistible, tantalizing men. Yes, *Man of the Month* will continue through 1991!

Man of the Month kicks off with *Nelson's Brand* by Diana Palmer. If you remember, Diana Palmer launched *Man of the Month* in 1989 with her fabulous book, *Reluctant Father*. I'm happy to say that *Nelson's Brand* is another winner—it's sensuous, highly charged and the hero, Gene Nelson, is a man you'll never forget.

But January is not only *Man of the Month*. This month, look out for additional love stories, starting with the delightful *Four Dollars and Fifty-One Cents* by Lass Small. And no, I'm not going to tell you what the title means—you'll have to read the book! There's also another great story by Carole Buck, *Paradise Remembered,* a sexy adventure by Jean Barrett, *Heat,* and a real charmer from Cathie Linz, *Handyman.* You'll also notice a new name, Ryanne Corey. But I'm sure you'll want to know that she's already written a number of fine romances as Courtney Ryan. Believe me, *The Valentine Street Hustle* is a winner!

As for February... well, I can't resist giving you a peek into next month. Get ready for *Outlaw* by Elizabeth Lowell! Not only is this a *Man of the Month*, it's also another powerful WESTERN LOVERS series.

You know, I could go on and on... but I'll restrain myself right now. Still, I will say that 1991 is going to be filled with wonderful things from Silhouette *Desire.* January *is just the beginning!*

All the best,
Lucia Macro
Senior Editor

LASS SMALL

FOUR DOLLARS AND FIFTY-ONE CENTS

SILHOUETTE *Desire*®

Published by Silhouette Books New York

America's Publisher of Contemporary Romance

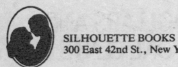

SILHOUETTE BOOKS
300 East 42nd St., New York, N.Y. 10017

FOUR DOLLARS AND FIFTY-ONE CENTS

ISBN: 0-373-05613-3

First Silhouette Books printing January 1991

Books by Lass Small

Silhouette Romance

An Irritating Man #444
Snow Bird #521

Silhouette Desire

Tangled Web #241
To Meet Again #322
Stolen Day #341
Possibles #356
Intrusive Man #373
To Love Again #397
Blindman's Bluff #413
Goldilocks and the Behr #437
Hide and Seek #453
Red Rover #491
Odd Man Out #505
Tagged #534
Contact #548
Wrong Address, Right Place #569
Not Easy #578
The Loner #594
Four Dollars and Fifty-One Cents #613

Silhouette Books

Silhouette Christmas Stories 1989
"Voice of the Turtles"

LASS SMALL

finds that living on this planet at this time is a fascinating experience. People are amazing. She thinks that to be a teller of tales of people, places and things is absolutely marvelous.

One

"We need one more man." Tabby allowed herself a small frown as she checked the time. "We can't just have four in the auction. We need a fifth. Someone, anyone, will be okay. How about a younger man? We can't leave until this is decided."

Silthy's comment was almost lost in the buzz of impatient voices. "What about Junior?"

A thoughtful, louder voice commented, "I'd forgotten about him. He is back in town again. Is he still running around loose?"

"Who?" someone inquired vaguely.

"Junior." Mary made the word boom out over their heads. "He lives next door to Janet. You remember him."

They all turned their heads and looked at Janet Folger, who bristled a little.

Tabby asked, "He isn't married yet, is he, Jan?"

"No," Jan replied in a brushing-aside way.

Mary asked, "Then why not ask him?"

Tabby said, "Good. That's settled."

Jan groused, "The invitation should come from the chairperson."

"Look, Jan, you live next door. Feel him out on this—" there were snorts and giggles "—and report back on Thursday. I've never been involved with anything that moved this sluggishly. We have to get on top of this and get it *done* or it won't work."

Jan asked, "How much should we make on the auction?"

"If we're lucky, we ought to clear about two thousand for the park tree plantings."

"It's a lot of hassle for two thousand."

"The purpose of our projects is community involvement. In other towns this idea of an auction has been used a lot and it always works. It's fun."

And a voice asked, "Who is going to bid on Junior?"

Before anyone else could say anything about Junior's lack of marketability, Jan said, "There's fifty-seven members of the Garden Club. If everyone volunteers to contribute—"

"Jan." Tabby's voice was excessively kind so that everyone knew she was being that way. "Do you have some problem about asking Junior to volunteer to be auctioned at the Mid-Summer Festival?" Her voice turned a little bit snide right at the end and rather spoiled the effect. Well, it was late, and they were all a little testy. But then Tabby ground in: "He is your neighbor."

Yeah. He'd lived next door almost all of their lives. When Jan was twelve, she'd briefly tried out her newly emerging womanly wiles on Junior. He hadn't noticed. Now, what had made her think of that? It was because she was going to have to ask him to allow himself the humiliation of being auctioned off to a whole roomful of indifferent women. "Tabby!" Jan said over the buzz.

"What!" There was real hostility there.

"I can't allow a neighbor to be put to the strain of a public auction. I grew up with Junior. He's never really fit in. He's only been back here about three months, and to ask him to do this wouldn't be kind."

That didn't earn Jan any brownie points. Her protest was lengthening the meeting and everyone wanted to go home. Tabby flared her eyes a little. As any really dedicated public-minded citizen knew, the problem had to be solved right then. She said with only a touch of terseness, "We'll have a silent auction. No one will know how much has been bid, except for the person appointed to read the bids."

"That won't work," Sue objected. "Not that *I* wouldn't trust a sister gardener, but there just might be some question as to who *really* made the top bid for Tad."

There were exclamations and laughter and…shouts of agreement. Tad was their drawing card. So the judging had to be solved with a three-member bid-reading committee—sworn to secrecy. That rider had been added after a kind soul proclaimed: "Junior ought not know his highest bid."

Then, when Tabby demanded to know why there were giggles over in the corner, a laughing voice asked, "Who'd bid on Junior, anyway? In school, he was so antisocial."

Tabby retorted in a hissingly strident voice, "All of us! The minimum bid we each have to place on every auctioned man is four dollars and fifty cents. Either volunteer that amount or be docked double the sum."

So just before the meeting was closed, Tabby pierced Jan with her chairperson's commanding look and told her, "Jan, you will contact Junior for his permission to enter his name in the lists."

The lists? That sounded like medieval combat, as if he was going to joust.

Well, Jan thought, in a way he would be. To set himself up to be bid on wouldn't be much fun for Junior. He'd never been in any of the main groups who did the current things, although he'd sometimes been on the edges. While he had dated, he hadn't been really... mainstream. And he was still single.

So was Jan.

Not quite five foot four, Jan had big blue eyes and long curling camel lashes. Junior had once told her the lashes looked like spider legs. She had something of an overbite, which gave her lips a bee-stung, ready look.

At twenty-four, Jan was still well within the marriage-potential years; at twenty-seven Junior was on the threshold of prime. He was built bulky and plain, not at all repulsive but not choice. Who would bid on him? Involved in road construction, he didn't even make himself available. He mostly worked. He worked and went to games and fished. That wasn't a man looking for a wife. Or a man who wanted to be auctioned off to some man-hunting woman.

With the meeting finally over, Jan drove her bunch home. She had always been the driver, even in high school. Now, it was because of the cost of gas. Back then, none of the other girls would drive because she might run across a boy who had a car, and she would desert Jan to let him take her home.

In those years, Jan had been followed home a couple of times, but who knew that? A really confident woman never mentioned who'd followed her home . . . especially since her father had come to open the door for her, always at the wrong time, and been cheerfully welcoming to her awkwardly budding Lothario. Daughters had it rough.

Two years ago, Jan's father had been transferred and her parents had moved from Indiana clear out to Colorado—and they were not planning to return permanently. That left the youngest of three sisters, Janet Folger, there in the town of Byford, Indiana, holding the bag, the bag being the family residence.

The house was an old red-brick monstrosity, decorated with limestone and sitting under a slate roof. Even before the preservation craze hit the Midwest, Byford cherished its beautiful houses and old buildings. Even the next echelon was being preserved. They weren't as attractive, but they did have a charm of their own.

The Folger house was one of those. It was roomy and airy and all the family celebrations were held there. That carried mixed blessings. At Christmas, Jan had accused her mother: "You planned it this way. You maneuvered for Dad to be transferred and to leave me stuck with the gatherings."

And her mother had smiled a cat smile and replied complacently, "Yes."

Jan drove onto her cracked cement driveway, back to the detached brick-sided, slate-roofed garage, where she got out, opened the heavy accordion doors and put her car away for the night.

Disgruntled, she looked over at Junior Busby's house, and there were no lights. It was after eleven; he was probably asleep. He led a predictable life.

Now, how was she going to have him do something so rash as to volunteer himself to be auctioned off in a competition in which he'd be ignored? It wasn't that she was concerned for him, but he had lived next door most of her life. Just in consideration for his feelings, didn't she owe him some loyalty? Although he'd never appeared to have any sensitivity, everyone had some sense of self-worth. His could be harmed.

Well, she'd ask. She wouldn't push, she'd just ask; and he'd say "No," just as he had for her eighth-grade dance when she'd been *desperate* for a partner. Really. Why was she worried about him? He would say no. There wasn't a problem.

Jan tried for three bloodily irritating days to get in touch with Junior. Then she got smart. What did any woman do in order to have a man contact her? She washed her hair. It *always* worked. One either washed her hair or got a horrific head cold. Washing her hair was easier.

So late on Saturday evening, she was sitting on the lower cement buttress by the cement front-porch stairs, drying her hair with a towel, when Junior came up the street and stopped.

Her head was buried in the towel, and he stood watching her. She was sitting cross-legged, bare-footed, dressed in an ankle-length cotton pullover that should have been shapeless but on her looked like a navy blue woman's body. The scooped neck showed a chain but whatever was on it was lost between her breasts, which jiggled nicely with her rubbing her hair.

She lowered the towel; her eyes were closed. She whirled her head back and forth, to whip her brown hair, and opened her blue eyes, looking through the mess of hair right into Junior's hazel eyes. She went blank.

He'd been visiting in the neighborhood. He was wearing a pair of shorts and a T-shirt. He was sweaty. She'd been looking at him in such irritation, through the recent hello's given in passing, that she hadn't really seen him. He might not have as much trouble in the bidding as she'd thought. Her bemused gaze went down his body in some surprise. Junior had matured. She looked back into his hazel eyes and said, "It always works."

"What?" A logical encouragement to such a statement.

She explained kindly, "If a woman wants to speak to a man, the last-ditch effort is to wash her hair."

"You only wash your hair when you want to talk to some guy?"

A typical Junior conversation. He hadn't changed. With patience that indicated her maturity, Jan replied, "I wanted to talk to you. I've tried to get hold of you for three days. Tabby is breathing down my neck. You know what sharp little teeth she has—"

"You got a cat. It's up a tree. You want me to get it down. No."

"No."

He frowned. "You feeling okay?"

"Junior." The second syllable was a shade higher than the first. She had tried to avoid ever doing that. His mother had called him that way for one hundred years, right next door, as he had grown up.

He put his hands low on his hips and just waited.

She thought he looked pretty good, standing there. She said more cheerfully, "I belong to the Garden Club, and as our part of the Mid-Summer Festival we're having an auction to raise money for tree plantings. You know how much that's needed, with the fires in the west and the deliberate burnings of the rain forests in the lower hemisphere?"

"How much?"

"No. You don't have to donate anything." She laughed a little. "Just your body. We're auctioning off men as dates for women bidders. You—"

"No."

See? It was easy. She'd approached him. He'd refused. She'd completed her mission. "It would be fun. And it's for a good cause." Good grief, she was still talking? Her tongue went on quite readily: "Tad is one. Paul is another who has agreed. You'd be in good company. Mickey thought it would be 'a kick.' And John even *asked* to be included. We don't ordinarily take volunteers, because we'd be swamped." That was an out-and-out lie. "He was on the list anyway, so we have him, too. We'd like you to—"

"No." He watched her take a deep calming breath. Then she leaned over and wrapped the towel around her head, stood up, tucked in the end and dropped her hands to her hips.

She looked exotic. The damp dark T-shirt dress clung down her and the chain with the hidden medallion caught his glance. He waited.

Realizing she had taken a belligerent stance, she modified it, crossing her arms over her chest. But that was just as bad, and finally she left her arms to just hang loose. Her tone was reasonable. "We all have to do our part in the preservation of forests."

He didn't reply. But he didn't leave, either.

So she said, "Please. We need one more man to volunteer for this auction."

"I thought you had to be careful about all the men who clamored to be included."

Uh. Yes. How nasty of him to keep track of conversations. "Someone mentioned that you hadn't been invited. At the meeting on Wednesday."

He shifted his feet and stood relaxed. "Are you nervous about this?"

"The auction?"

"No. About asking me to do this?"

"Not at all." Lying came easily when the alternative was telling the truth. "I volunteered to contact you since you live next door."

"But it wasn't your idea to invite me to do this?"

She licked her lips quickly and betrayed the fact that she would bend the truth. "Your name came up—"

"Who told you to ask me?"

"You live next door—" He had very compelling eyes. The different colors were fascinating.

He gestured, clarifying the premise. "I get up like a slave on the block and nobody bids."

"It's a silent auction. The bids come in after the first gathering and—"

"First...gathering?" It was obvious that he wasn't thrilled.

"Yes. So the women can look you over and decide which one they want and how high they'll go to get you."

"You going to bid?"

She was businesslike but gentle. "The committee members will put in base bids on each man."

"So. Whoever gets me, gets me at rock-bottom bidding."

"Oh, no," she soothed. "Women will be competing. Of course, Tad will be the prime draw. Uh. So will you. You're very nice-looking...and...well-made."

"I can also walk and talk."

Tartly, she retorted, "I really wouldn't know about that. I haven't seen much of you lately."

"You never could."

She gave him a spark-shooting glance and didn't exhale. But she stayed calm. "Just come to the initial meeting on Monday evening. It's a light supper for the committee and the volunteers. After that, everyone is invited to view the volunteers as they are introduced, and hear how the festival will be scheduled. It's only five dollars."

For clarity, he tacked words onto her sentence: "—for a 'light' supper."

"The committee is serving it, and we have to meet expenses."

"My truck's in the shop." He watched her with his head tilted back. "I'll go with you."

"I hadn't planned on coming home first."

"Then I'll meet you there, and you can drive me home afterward."

He gave her a nasty look of command so that she didn't dare disagree, since he had *almost* agreed to be auctioned. So she nodded reluctantly.

But on Sunday night, Jan heard Junior's truck leave his driveway, and she frowned into the darkness. His truck was in the shop; therefore, he would have to ride home with her after the meet the next evening. Hadn't he said that?

The next day at Benton's Office Machinery and Supplies, Jan called Tabby. "I think Junior will go with it."

"Is he coming tonight?"

"Yes."

"That nails him." Tabby's tone was satisfied. "We'll see to it that he's trapped and has to do it. Leave it to me."

Jan hung up the phone slowly, a little uneasy to abandon an innocent Junior to a practiced Tabby. But, hell, he was twenty-seven. He would be able to take care of himself. And if he couldn't, coping with Tabby was good experience. Clawed up, even Junior could survive. Actually it would be interesting to see the stubborn, uncooperative Junior *cope* with a determined Tabby.

Jan smiled out of her office window at the brick building next door. What if Junior had just driven away last night and . . . escaped?

She tried to call him, and his secretary at the construction company said he wasn't where he could be reached. What kind of a secretary said things like that? Was he just out of the office? Or was he safely out of Byford and on the moon? What did it matter to her?

But she spent the entire day sweating if Junior would be anywhere around for her to snatch come suppertime and the meeting. Men were a dreadful nuisance. And Junior Busby had never been very helpful. Just wait until Tabby got her fingernails into Junior. Hah!

If he hadn't escaped.

She was so distracted that she had trouble with her computer, which didn't seem to be able to adjust to her. Stupid machine.

She'd fixed a frozen fruit salad in gelatin to take to the supper. It had melted a little in the freezer at the office and it didn't look . . . fresh. Jan closed her eyes and was enduring. One eventually learned to adjust to things that went awry. Her mother had said so.

She got to the meeting hall just off the hotel lobby and immediately dodged Tabby so that she could get Mildred to quick-freeze the salad in the hotel freezer. Mildred didn't cooperate. "Our freezer is full. This time of year, we serve things that go in there. We don't have room for a whole lot of stuff brought in from people's houses. Why didn't you have us do this supper?"

"We have a very slim budget. We're working on planting trees. I'm being staunch. Don't rattle me."

"Jan, you're such a pushover."

In astonishment, Jan watched Mildred walk away. A pushover? But Mildred was carrying off Jan's semifrozen salad. Then, still staunch, Jan went in search of the elusive Junior.

She stood at the entrance. He didn't show up. She got to greet everyone else and people tried to get her to do all sorts of errands, but she was still being staunch and declined, saying apologetically, "I have to be here when Junior shows up."

Someone finally told her, "Junior's at the bar having a beer."

Jan looked out the door at nothing while she calmed down, then she went into the bar and found Junior surrounded by a pack of men who were discussing something dumb like fishing. Or was it soccer? And she noted that he was still in his work clothes, denims with a hard hat attached to a shoulder tab on his jacket. Yes. She reached a hand through the mass of bodies and clutched Junior.

The men were all strangers. They eyed Jan and smiled and laughed at Junior. He looked patient and not very agreeable. He didn't smile. She said, "We need you for the pictures."

His eyes went opaque as he said, "Pictures?" in such a way that Jan knew she had another problem.

She smiled at the hampering barricade of men and said, "Will you excuse us? They're waiting for Junior."

The men laughed heartily and questioned, "Junior?"

"She goes back to my childhood," he explained.

But he did extricate himself from his buddies, and he did accompany her to the meeting room where tables had been set up for the light, pre-preview supper. She told him with remarkable patience, "I already bought your supper ticket."

"Fine."

He didn't offer to reimburse her.

They went through the line and selected their choices from the bowls and platters on the serving tables. Someone had brought a garden bouquet and the table was very pretty. Junior asked Jan to carry his extra plate. This was no light supper for him. She was a little embarrassed by his gluttony.

He ate with purpose, but he didn't throw the bones over his shoulder onto the floor. He put them back on the plate. So he had learned something since she'd last been with him. He didn't talk at all.

All the other men came nicely dressed, and everyone else chatted and laughed. Tad was at the center of a group of women and he loved it. So did they. Jan decided she was going to take her grandmother's five-hundred-dollar bequest and put it on her bid for Tad.

If she could have Tad to herself during the festival, he would see that she would make him a perfect wife.

Jan noted there were women who might have joined Junior. They hesitatingly gave greetings to Jan and waited to catch Junior's eye, but they were ignored by him.

With continuing "staunch," Jan stood by him in order to make him seem a desirable part of the group. And after he'd been back to the buffet table a second time, he said, "Let's go."

"The business hasn't been discussed yet," she mentioned.

"What business?"

"The auction."

"I agreed." He opened his hand out minimally.

"You . . . we have to discuss it."

"What's there to discuss?"

"The . . . arrangements."

"What arrangements?" He eyed her suspiciously.

"The pictures and things."

"Pictures?"

She moved one hand by her shoulder in an attempt to dismiss that touchy subject. "So people can read about the auction and make bids."

"You didn't say anything about this being in the *Bugle*."

"And in the Fort Wayne papers, too."

"No." He was adamant.

"You agreed."

"I'm leaving. Forget this."

"Tabby!" Jan yelled at the ceiling.

And Tabby appeared like magic. "Oh, Junior!" she said as if she'd been searching for him for *weeks*! And if Jan could have just organized herself and quit panicking, she could have learned a lot, right then, about handling a man who was recalcitrant.

Tabby tucked her hand into the crook of Junior's denimed arm and hugged it against her softness. Jan noted that and saw Junior's ears point. Fascinating. He turned his head down to look at Tabby, and his ears pointed. And Tabby said, "We'll let the photographer practice on you. You take such good pictures that then he'll be able to make the other men look almost as good."

Jan heard Tabby say that. And Jan believed it, just like Junior. He lifted his head arrogantly and looked around at the masses, dismissing them all as he said to Tabby, "Okay. Let's get it over with." Then he pinned Jan with a glance and told her, "Don't move. Wait here."

And she found herself doing just that.

Every other women there crowded around the photographer and teased the man who was being filmed under the lights. The men were all laughing and posing and looking their best and most flattered. It was brilliantly done. Who wouldn't respond to a little flattery?

Junior didn't.

He stared at the camera as if he wanted to know it. Then he slowly winked.

Who saw that besides Jan?

Then Junior decided he had had enough and he simply left the group and came to where he'd told Jan to stay. And she was there. Again he said to her, "Let's go."

"You don't know when you're supposed to be where."

"You can tell me." He said that as they were walking out of the hotel.

She protested: "I *can't* tell you. I can never find you to tell you!" She was indignant.

As they went through the lobby Mildred met them, holding a dish, and she told Jan, "Here's your salad."

Jan gave her a neutral look, which showed how adult she was, and she said only, "Thank you." And she took the full, untouched dish to the car.

He asked, "What's that?"

"You don't want to know."

"It isn't somebody's brain or anything, is it?"

"I believe I could acquire a distaste for you."

He laughed.

She took him home, stopped in front of his house and simply waited.

"You're not going to walk me to the door?"

With raveling patience, she replied, "No."

"I am disappointed in you, Miss Folger. Your parents would be ashamed of you."

"Probably."

"You make that sound like it might not be the same shame that I would have them feel," he told her.

"Probably."

"When is the next meeting?"

"I don't know."

"That might not be an honest reply," he speculated.

"Probably."

And he had the gall to laugh.

She didn't wait to see if he got safely into his house. She really didn't give a damn. She drove into her own driveway, put her car safely into the garage vault that protected it, went into her house and had a long, hot shower. Then she crawled into her bed and went over the whole evening in her mind, with emphasis on several conversations, before she got up, took two aspirin and went back to bed.

But she had to get up again, go down to the garage and retrieve the rotting, unfrozen fruit salad and carry it into the house to dump it into the garbage.

The phone rang, but any woman living alone never answers the phone late at night. The callers either make salacious remarks or animal sounds.

So then came a knocking on her front door. Jan went to the open window above the porch and yelled, "Get away from my porch or I'll call the police, you pervert!"

"Oh hell," said Junior's voice. "What were you doing outside that late?"

"I go out all the time. Haven't you ever noticed?"

"No," he replied. "I sleep on the other side of my house."

"How nice for Mrs. Witherspoon." She was Junior's other next-door neighbor.

"Are you all right?"

"Yes."

"It was an interesting evening," he called up at her window from the middle of her front yard.

Mrs. Thompson hollered from across the street, "We're all glad you enjoyed it. Why don't you go to bed?"

He had the brashness to exclaim, "Why, Mrs. Thompson! What are you suggesting?"

The old lady sputtered.

And Jan slammed the window closed.

After that, silence reigned . . . except for the whistling that came from Junior as he crossed Jan's yard and went on over to his own.

Men! Jan went downstairs and drank a glass of cold milk and paced around inside her house for an hour before she settled down enough to go back to bed.

Two

Immediately on wakening, Jan went out and searched for her morning paper. It wasn't on her porch or in the yard. She called the *Bugle* to complain, and Temple said, "It was, too, delivered. You just want a free copy of the men's pictures."

Jan said with restraint, "I did not receive the *Bugle* today."

"Somebody must be stealing them. You're the fifth complaint so far."

"I don't know what happened to my copy, but I want my paper," Jan told her. "I bought and paid for it, and I want each copy of the paper as it is printed."

"Okay, okay, okay. We'll put it inside your front door. Leave it open, Jan. But we can't get it there until ten o'clock. Wait'll you see the picture of Junior!"

"Thank you." As Jan hung up, she decided she was going to move to a big city where people were always polite to each other. There, she would know no one and wouldn't have to put up with any back talk.

She dressed, had breakfast, drove downtown and bought every different paper as it came onto the stands.

Junior dominated the whole page in the *Bugle*. He was at the bottom, and his picture was just of his face and chest. He wasn't as well-known as the other men, so he hadn't been featured as Tad had been. But there was no question that Junior dominated the page.

The other four looked cheerful and pleasant, well-dressed and easy. They were laughing as if what they were doing was fun and the viewer was included in the adventure. Any one of those four would snare in bids from any viewing women.

Then there was the picture of Junior. He was in denims with that hard hat hanging off his shoulder at his back. He hadn't shaved as the other men must have, so his beard showed faintly. And it was he who jarred the women who would be studying the men to be auctioned.

He looked as if he was looking right at her and he was winking. It was a serious wink, not flirting or sassy. It was a deadly serious wink. It was the kind that lured women into doing something unthinkably wicked... like bidding on a man who was an unpredictable unknown.

And after staring at Junior for some time, Jan realized that the picture had to be a great relief to her. She knew some rash women would bid on Junior and therefore her club-dunned four dollars and fifty cents were safe. She could concentrate all her resources on bidding for Tad. Why not try for the best? She was worthy of Tad.

She looked okay. Well, her breasts were placed a little too close together. Her hair was a mouse brown. Her top teeth protruded a trifle. But she was clean, neat and orderly, and she used a deodorant.

She had practiced all but one of the skills needed to be a good wife and mother. She'd done volunteer work in a child-care center, thereby contracting a case of head lice that were making the rounds again that year in all the lower grades.

She knew how to sew and mend. She could cook, not always very successfully, but she was adventuresome and aware of what was appealing to the eye and palate. She was tidy.

She could be a man's pal. She could drink a whole beer. She didn't flinch in putting a worm on a hook, although given a choice, she'd rather not do that. She could fire a gun without closing her eyes, and she generally hit where she aimed.

Although she didn't understand hockey, she didn't mind football, but she tended to doze through baseball. She didn't like speed bicycles, but other than that she was willing to swim or hike or camp out. Well, she did refuse to hang glide and she couldn't watch. Heights disoriented her.

But as long as a man stayed on fairly level ground, she was the perfect mate. If she could be around Tad for a while and he had the time to really ''see'' her, he would recognize that. He would be worth the five hundred dollars, and her grandmother would approve of Jan spending the money in that way. And since the money would go to new trees, it would help the environment.

Jan sat at her desk, confidently calm and, as an observer, she viewed the layouts of the other papers.

One Fort Wayne paper was very irritating. The female photographer had gotten carried away with Junior and featured him. How like a paper that didn't know the local story.

But that was good! Concentrate all the attention on someone else, and that left Tad's appeal relatively local. That way, Jan's five hundred ought to do the trick. Jan would win Tad. It was in the book to happen exactly that way.

Jan's smile was something very similar to Tabby's most contented one.

At noon that day, the usual phalanx of women met at Dorothy's Do Drop Inn to exchange gossip and have lunch. And just *everybody* was talking about Junior!

"Those eyes!" one moaned.

"That body!" another sighed.

Jan pointed out logically, "You can only see his head and chest."

But that only elicited groans about his chest. They discussed his eyebrows, his eyelashes and his mouth. That did not make any sense at all to Jan.

She listened with growing hostility, but gradually that turned to dismay. The newspaper pictures had been so misleading that these women now thought of Junior as a hero type! How could they be so misled? They'd known him all their lives. What was the matter with them?

They were going to bid on him.

The panicky feeling in Jan's chest was distracting until she realized that she felt responsible for her neighbor. He was being figuratively thrown to the lionesses, and he'd be shown up as the klutz he was.

That was not Jan's responsibility.

While that was so, and while he had never stepped in when she had needed him, she was a Samaritan, committed to the rescue of beleaguered people, plants and animals. Junior did fit in one of those categories, if one didn't catalogue too severely.

Jan faced the fact that she was going to have to do something to rescue Junior. She sighed in disgust and looked out the sparkling window. It was up to Jan. Why did these things always have to happen to her? Why was she always the one left to pick up the mangy dog and get it to the animal shelter? Now she had to do something similar for Junior.

She barely tasted her food. But she did eat. She needed all the vitality she could get in order to cope with what lay ahead of her. She had no trouble leaving Dorothy's because no one ever paid any attention to her comings and goings.

At her office she sat at her desk, girding her loins before dialing his office number. Disgruntled, she waited for him to reply, and got his secretary again. "Is Junior there?"

"Mr. Busby is unavailable. May I ask who's calling?"

"Never mind." Jan never could just hang up. It would be rude.

His secretary volunteered, "You wouldn't believe the women who've been calling here, today. Must be the picture!" And she laughed.

Jan didn't think it was at all funny. But then, the secretary's laugh wasn't amused, it was . . . excited.

She was another who suddenly thought that Junior was the be-all and end-all. Where had they been all this time? What did they see in him now that hadn't been

there all along? Nothing. Just a picture in a newspaper, and they attributed all sorts of magic to him.

So his secretary's comment surprised Jan. "You'd
think they didn't know him when he's lived here most
of his life. Where've they been?"

"Yeah," Jan agreed. "Tell him Jan called and I
have to see him . . . about the auction."

His secretary began a chortle.

With the sighing patience of a put-upon female Job,
Jan elaborated: "I'm on the committee."

"Oh. That's a new approach. I'll put you on the
list."

No man should have such a forward secretary. What
had happened to a businesslike approach? But Jan *had*
learned that women weren't waiting for the formality
of the auction, they had already started to besiege poor
Junior. Jan would have to begin immediately to sal-
vage him so that he wouldn't disillusion any of the
bidders.

Holding Mrs. Witherspoon's cat on her lap, Jan was
sitting, dozing on his back steps rather late, when Junior finally got home. He ran the car onto the neglected grass and got out tiredly. Then he looked over
at her house, stretched and straightened his old baseball cap before he turned and saw her sitting there in
the early moonlight. He paused, relaxed, his eyes
going to slits, and he smiled a little.

She mentioned, "You ought not park on the grass,
you'll kill it."

"What you want?"

Now, how was she going to approach the subject of
the reeducation of Junior Busby? She asked, "Why
did your parents name you Junior? You're not named

after your father. They just named you Junior. Why did they do that?''

He looked aside as he pulled on his earlobe, then he looked at her and raised his thick, straight brows as he replied, ''I don't know.''

''You've just been called that?''

''My friends call me J.R.''

She stared. He was just like those pictures in the paper.

Helpfully he continued, ''It's the abbreviation of Junior.'' Then he added, ''J, R.''

''We have a lot to do before the auction dinner and dance.'' She could not prevent a sigh of resignation. ''It's going to take a lot of time and patience.'' She emphasized that quite earnestly. ''Do you dance at all?''

''A little.''

''Did your parents teach you any of the social graces? I don't remember ever seeing any evidence of that.''

He licked his lips and replied soberly, ''Not that I recall.''

''You have to know that this auction carries the entire weight of the reputation of the Garden Club on its shoulders. You understand that? If you turn out to be an embarrassment, the club would suffer for it.''

''Holy Moses,'' he exclaimed aghast. ''What *can* I do?''

''Junior, you have just given me hope that you will cooperate in this endeavor. And it isn't entirely for the club that I am willing to help you. Although you never helped *me* out in any crisis, I do feel an obligation toward—''

"When didn't I help you? I buried that damned cat of yours that was squashed on the stre—"

In high horror she retorted, "You carried Sugar by her *tail!*"

"Now, Janet—"

With a great recovery, reached for and attained with remarkable inner struggle, Jan said firmly, "Sugar is neither here nor there. The reason I'm—"

"She's floating between heaven and hell?"

By biting her lower lip, Jan found the patience and restrained herself from giving a scathing reply or flouncing away. "Junior, this is serious. Please. I am trying to help you."

He slowly, unthreateningly climbed the few steps and sat down on the step above her. From there, he looked down at her, seeing past her eyelashes and that little nose, down the slight gap in her blouse to the chain that held some mysterious something inside her blouse, secreted between her nice, round breasts.

She looked up at him, and they gazed at each other for a time. He slowly licked his lips and that broke her stare, for she had to watch that marvelous accomplishment. He did that very well. But a man couldn't spend an entire evening licking his lips. He needed some of the social graces.

Prissily she commented, "I noticed yesterday that you at least didn't throw the chicken bones on the floor. So we don't have to start quite from scratch."

"Did I ever tell you how relieved I was when you gave up on that Parson rat? I didn't know what in God's name you ever saw in him."

"Maryetta Teller caught his eye. He gave me up."

"You made a lucky escape."

"It did turn out that way, but you might have mentioned it at the time. You never said a word."

"I talked myself blue in the face, trying to make you listen to me. He was rotten."

"When did you ever say anything? You never did give an opinion!"

"You hit me with the bicycle pump! Want to see the scar?"

She looked at him startled. A scar? Where? "Oh, yes. I remember." And she blushed.

"Well, congratulations. Now, how are you going to teach me manners?" He hit the "you" so lightly that it turned out to be just for his own amusement.

Jan thought he appeared commendably receptive. That was a plus. But how to begin? "Do you have any idea what to do, so that I can judge where you need the most help?"

He took some time in replying. He stood up and turned his back to her and used both hands to rub his face.

And Janet suddenly realized that he wasn't just the irritating boy-next-door, but a human being and that she might have offended him. Even with the best possible intentions, she must have seemed unduly critical. That could seem degrading. And her heart went out to him. "Junior—"

"Try J.R."

"J.R., I didn't mean you're a Neanderthal. I only want to help you. You're my neighbor. I was the one who recruited you. All the women are raving over that picture of you in the paper and—"

"They are?"

"Yes," she bravely admitted. "And I wouldn't be at all surprised if some of them bid on you. You want to make a good impression. So let me help you to learn to dance and not make any major faux pas."

"Faux pas. I haven't heard that in a while."

"It means mistakes."

He nodded. "If you don't mind, we'll have to begin another time. Not tonight. I'm dead on my feet. Construction work goes with the daylight hours. Winters I'm a little livelier. I couldn't dance a step tonight. I've eaten, so you can't monitor my table manners, but I can walk you home and see if that's okay. Okay?"

"Yes. I do understand, but we haven't too much time. The festival is in three weeks. The announcement dance is only two and a half weeks from now. It really is vital that any chance be used to help you out."

"Miss Folger, may I escort you to your house?" He held out his hand.

She removed the cat from her lap, took his hand and said, "Thank you."

He hauled too hard, and she tripped off the step, falling against him. He caught her and struggled backward, staggering to retain his equilibrium, clutching her closely. Puffing, he explained, "I've been guiding beams all day and they weigh more than you. You're a feather." He finally set her on her feet, his arm brushing her breasts. "Sorry."

She nodded, understanding that the arm-brushing had been unavoidable. She smiled a little, then laughed. "I don't think you need to practice flattery. You did that very well."

"Why...thank you, Miss Folger."

"You're welcome, J.R. Now, take my elbow and guide me over the uneven ground."

"Uneven? I rolled the lawn this spring!"

"This is practice. Women are generally wearing heels, and they don't walk too steadily. Men always watch their way for them and take their arm so they won't break their necks."

"And sue?"

"Right."

"Good thing you warned me. Watch the hedge. Here, let me hold it back. Now, how was that?"

"Well done."

"And the steps?" he inquired with interest.

"You help me up them the same way, and you take my key and unlock the door."

"Give me the key."

"It isn't locked. We're pretending."

"And?"

"You say good-night and that you'll call. And you do call the next day and tell the lady how much you enjoyed her company."

"When do I kiss her?"

Jan was stunned. J.R. would kiss the woman. Jan hadn't thought about that. "Well, I don't believe . . . I don't know. I don't think you ought to rush that part on the first date."

"What if she insists?"

Any woman who bid good money on a man could very well expect him to kiss her. "I doubt you need any instruction on that."

"The only thing I know to do is to try it out on you, because I know damned good and well you'll tell me if I'm any good or if I need to practice that, too."

Her gaze flicked to his face and her tongue stumbled over itself as the most amazing shiver went through her body at the thought of Junior kissing her. It had to be revulsion. But it really was a rather thrilling quivering. She said a little too quickly, "Uh. Not this first time."

"With the next date?" He stood there perfectly in control, his face serious and attentive, ready to be instructed in this phase of life . . . by her.

She didn't know that much about the whole process. She was no real authority on kissing. She'd had some very pleasant exchanges, but she didn't have any advanced degrees in it. She found a word and used it: "Maybe."

"Okay," he said quite cheerfully, as he took her arm and tugged her toward the steps. "Let's go back and try it all again. You be critical, but don't give me any hints or suggestions."

She trembled. He wanted instructions on how to conduct himself on the second date. He was maneuvering for that. It scared something inside her and she mumbled, "Uh. Not tonight." Then her tongue hurried along and began to run with it. "I know how exhausted you must be. You did very well. We need to share a meal, so that I can watch your table manners. And we need to dance together. We need to do those things so that you can . . . well, so that you'll . . . fit in all right and be comfortable."

He shook his head once halfway, impressed with her, and said, "You're a good neighbor. Not everyone would take the time to help a guy this way. It shows that you have a good character."

Earnestly she assured him, "I do want you to enjoy this."

"I'll love it." He grinned.

"Yes," she said rather sadly. And she knew that he would. He picked up on things very quickly. The two and a half weeks would probably be enough. She knew exactly how he should act and he had shown that he could adjust beautifully. He would be a perfect gentleman by then. The woman whose bid won him for the festival would be in her glory with him as her escort.

"Good night." He watched her.

"Yes." She went past him, through her opened screened door and turned back.

In his no-nonsense voice, he told her, "Lock it."

"Yes." She did that, then reluctantly closed the other door, shutting him out. She stood there, listening, as he whistled his way home.

The next day at her office J.R. called her from a phone booth along a highway, and through the roar of traffic he yelled, "Miss Folger, I just wanted to say what a pleasure it was to walk you home last night."

And she laughed low and amused in her throat, in a sound that was very strange to her ears. "You catch on very nicely, J.R. You did well."

"We need to get the other aspects of the male/female intercourse done. Social intercourse, you understand?"

Her gasp had caused him to back up and explain. So his correction had been necessary to sort out her mind, and she turned as scarlet as her instant, lasciviously enticing visions.

J.R. then yelled to the side, "I'm on my way, damn it, let up a while! Goodbye, Miss Folger. I'll be in touch."

But he hung up without giving her a chance to say anything.

Everyone Jan talked to in the next couple of days talked about J.R. and the festival, in that order. That depressed her. She figured the resulting melancholy was because time was passing and she hadn't had any contact with J.R. to help him appear smooth and practiced. But he'd done very well with the first lesson.

So it was three days later when she drove into her driveway and found him lounging on her back porch. He rose and walked over to her car to open her door, then gave her his hand to help her out as he said, "Let's go out and eat. I know a barn that serves great ribs, and they have an old jukebox. We can begin the dancing instruction."

"I think you're being very mature about all this, Jun—J.R."

"And you're being very neighborly."

"Thank you."

"You're really going to be welcome."

She frowned a little over that particular wordage, but she asked, "Am I suitably dressed?"

He had the excuse to look down her body, as he pretended to evaluate her clothing. "You need to wear jeans and boots. Got any boots?"

"Wellingtons."

"Nary a rain cloud in sight. Wear your sneakers. And besides the jeans, you ought to wear a top of some kind."

She gave him a patient look and said, "I will."

"I wouldn't mind, you understand, but Ralph or Fred might not see eye to eye with you... looking somewhere else that way, you understand."

She pinched her lips together and promised, "I shall wear a top."

"Well, damn. No sense of adventure. You never did have any, but I thought you might develop one."

"I was first, going into the Psmythes' house after it had been vacant for ten years."

"It hadn't been ten years."

"You *said* so!"

"Yeah, but who can trust a Busby's word?"

She nodded twice in thoughtful agreement.

"Go change," he said. "I'll drive."

She looked with distaste over into his yard at his filthy pickup again parked on the grass. "Let me drive."

"No. Your clean car would look out of place. One wants to blend in, you must realize. I'll help you in my world, and you help me in the world of ladies' auctions."

His manner and word choice did catch her attention. It showed an openness that she hadn't realized J.R. Busby possessed. It really touched her that such a big, rough man could understand that he needed smoothing and polishing. It showed he was open to instruction and change. It was a milestone in their relationship, because he'd always been so damned stubborn that he'd exasperated the liver out of her most of their lives. Her impulse was to congratulate him, but she was sensitive to the fact that she should tread carefully for his sake, so she only said, "All right," and went on to change.

She emerged from her house in jeans and tennies. Her blouse was silk and she carried a cashmere sweater against the June evening's coolness. Her hair was loose and a little tumbled by her hurry. Her eyes were bright with this new adventure, and the chain still lay mostly hidden beneath her shirt.

The Barn was some distance, and Jan was quietly starving by the time they arrived. It was aptly named and sat as the only surviving building on what appeared to be an abandoned farm. It looked ratty. They drove onto the field in which the Barn rested so comfortably off-kilter, and J.R. parked in the weeds. There was one light above the regular size door.

They got out of the pickup and approached as the door was opened. Two rough-looking men emerged and cheerfully greeted J.R. by name. Jan wondered: where had he found such acquaintances?

Inside, the diverse clientele was familiar with her escort and yelled, "Hey, J.R." Even the women greeted him that way and were as casually loud. And the two had a beer. While Jan could drink one with a meal, drinking one on an empty stomach exhilarated her a little—so that she laughed a good deal and was a lot of fun.

She didn't mind that J.R. didn't move at all when he danced. He just held her and swayed a little to the beat. It was nice. She thought of the auction coming up. To avoid being docked the double amount, Jan had placed the prerequisite four-dollars-and-fifty-cents bid on J.R., with a penny extra because he was her neighbor. She felt perfectly safe because her own bid was now placed on Tad, and she couldn't claim two winners. She wished J.R. was Tad, and that she was dancing in Tad's arms and enjoying being so close.

It wasn't long now until the auction. Not very much longer, and dancing in Tad's arms wouldn't be a dream but reality.

Three

J.R. asked in a husky voice, "Why's that sly little smile on your mouth?"

Jan raised those camel lashes with some effort and replied to her neighbor, in whose arms she nestled as they stood to the music, "I bid grandmother's five hundred on Tad."

His smile had appeared with the first of her words and vanished entirely with the last one. "The whole kaboodle?" He was astounded.

"Yes."

"On . . . Tad?" His voice squeaked up in disbelief.

"I figure if he could get to know me, he'd be . . ."

"Be?"

She blushed.

He probed: "Be?"

"Perhaps he could see me in a . . . an individual way."

"You're interested in...Tad?" J.R. was having trouble with the idea.

"He's a fine person."

"Yeah. But not for a firebrand like you."

"Firebrand?" Her voice sounded reasonably close to the indignation she ought to be feeling, but her ego loved the label.

"Janet, you've been a hellcat all your life, and you could shock the *liver* out of a lily-livered nincompoop like Tad."

"That is your insulting opinion." She bristled.

"Remember Parson."

"I was younger then."

"Getting desperate at age twenty-four? Hearing the old bio clock ticking? Tired of getting up and going to work? Want a meal ticket? *Tad?*"

She pushed back from J.R.'s embrace and stood alone. "You are discouraging me. No gentleman talks that way to a lady. There is more to be done on you than I would *ever* have guessed. Is it possible for you to take a couple of days off?"

"I'll see what I can do." They stood there in the dark barn amid the roar of conversation. There was loud music and shouts among the shuffling bodies that bounced or barely moved to the country beat. The two were facing each other very seriously. J.R. inquired, "Are you telling everybody that you're betting five hundred on Tad? Somebody will put in an extra dollar and steal him away from you."

"You mean, 'outbid.'" She was a stickler.

"Yeah."

"No. You are the only one I've ever told that to, and in my past experience you've always been quite reliable with secrets. You never told about Pete playing doctor with me."

"I've always been so shocked that *Janet Folger* would have done anything like that, that I knew no one would ever believe me, or I would have told it. As it was, with a goody-goody like you, if I'd talked about you and Pete, people would have thought I was just being mean."

"You're shaking my faith in your discretion," she warned direly. "If I hear one word about how much I've bid on Tad, I'll know the source and take serious countermeasures."

"Like what?"

"I can't believe you'd blab on me, so I have no current plans for revenge."

"Current? You've had such in the past? Why?"

"All sorts of reasons, but none because you ever told."

"What about the committee? You trust them to be quiet? They're women!"

"You—" she took a steadying breath "—are implying that women can't keep secrets? If men only knew what all we *don't* tell."

"And the committee is sworn to silence? What paragons did you find to burden with this weighty trust?"

"Carol Meece, Peggy Starbuck and Minna Walters."

"Yeah. They're pristine. I respect them."

She slowly tilted up her head in a somewhat dangerous manner and looked into his lash-shaded hazel eyes. "How happy they would be to know they have your respect." But her snide tone was oddly gentle. She was a little distracted by the fact that even in the dim light of the barn dance floor, the hazel jewels of his eyes were discernible.

In the smoky voice that had recently begun to plague him, J.R. told her, "It's time for you to go home, Buttercup, on this, our second date."

"Date? These aren't dates. And we didn't eat properly. No one can eat ribs and french fries with a knife and fork without looking strange. This was simply... simply..." Her lifted hand circled in agitation, as she sought the word.

"A conference?" he supplied that helpfully.

"Consultation," she amended.

"All that we've talked about is Tad's lack of charisma and your dark past."

"Tad has a great many good friends." Her voice was gentle.

"Name two."

"Tabby Gates and Phyllis Minor."

"Men friends?"

"I see him only in crowds," she explained.

"Men don't like him. You need a man who has male friends, too. They generally know about plumbing and motors and things like that. Men friends are important."

"There are people who make their living repairing and correcting house fixtures and car innards."

"Innards?" He squinted.

"Viscera?"

In astonishment he realized: "You consider your car a creature?"

She nodded. "With an obtuse personality."

"You need a new car."

"How could I relinquish Tootie to a stranger?"

"To be crushed into a cube."

"You're really very nasty," she declared. "That trait doesn't show in your pictures."

He tilted his head. "You been looking at the newspapers?"

"I glanced through to see how Tad was presented. I . . . didn't want him to show up too well. It would excite other women into bidding."

"He looks like Charlie McCarthy."

"Edgar Bergen's dummy? That's really insulting. Saying that makes you sound . . . jealous."

J.R. laughed. "Come on, Petunia, it's time we got home and into our own little bed."

The thought of going to bed with him rattled her and she missed a step.

"Still feeling that one beer?" He put one arm supportively around her and took her near hand firmly in his. "You okay?"

"Release me. I am perfectly all right."

"Are you a roisterer? Do you sing when you're drunk? Or do we break up the place? There's a mirror behind the bar. I have dibs on that."

"Good grief, Junior—J.R. I am perfectly sober. And I cannot allow you to be destructive. Such publicity! It would be in all the papers! It would be adverse for any bidders on you, and it could even reflect on the Garden Club."

"I was only showing you how open-minded I am. I'm willing to participate. That's important in an escort."

She gave him a fishy look. Just what sort of "participation" did he have in mind? And the worry nagged at her about allowing him loose among some of the women she'd heard were going to bid on him.

They were vultures! They would strip his flesh from his bones and might even take his virtue.

J.R. took her through the noisy crowd to the exit from the Barn. In the darkness they found his dirty pickup among the haphazardly parked vehicles resting amid the bent and trampled weeds. He handed her into the truck with great skill. He was so smooth doing it that Jan wondered if he might not be quite practiced. When he had gone around the car and gotten into the driver's seat, she asked suspiciously, "Have you dated a good deal?"

"Not a good deal."

"You put me into the car in a very smooth way."

"Why, thank you, Janet."

"What did you do those years you spent out west in Albuquerque?"

"Worked my tail off."

"What made you come back to Byford and buy your house back from the Sniders?"

He drove with skill, but was silent for a minute, then he suggested, "There's no place like home?"

"You're rather glib. You reply without really telling anything."

"I'm honest."

"You don't run around with any of the people I know. What do you do with your time?"

"Work."

"Have you some goal? Some challenge? Are you aiming at something specifically? You're of an age to marry. What is your purpose in working so hard? I never see you." She bit her tongue. That last sentence sounded as if . . . she wanted to see him.

He glanced over at her and smiled. "I am structuring my life."

"That sounds like big plans."

"No. I am aiming for contentment."

She became pensive. "I understand that. I never dreamed my parents and my sisters would leave Byford. I thought we'd all live here, see each other and call each other and have a monthly meal together. That the grandchildren would know one another. It hasn't worked out that way for me, either."

"You have to remember I was an only child. I have no siblings to be nostalgic about. I have some great friends, good hard work, prospects. I'll make some lucky woman a hell of a good husband."

She looked over at him. He had a secret smile on his mouth, as he watched the road coming toward them in the headlights. She asked in a startled way, "Do you have some particular woman in mind?"

"I'm considering."

"Will...she...bid on you?"

"We'll see."

"Do you date her?"

"Not yet."

"Does she know of your...interest in her?"

"Not yet."

"Well. I believe it would be best if you'd indicate to her that you are interested." The words had been rather stilted and slow, then they came in a rush: "Who is she?"

"I'll let her know in plenty of time."

"In time...for what?"

"So she isn't surprised by the honeymoon."

"Oh." It was a rather sad little word. It went out of her mouth and seemed to just sit on the dashboard, drawing both their attentions to it. "Do I...know her?"

"Yes."

"Oh." That one went and sat with the other "oh" on the dashboard. She glanced back at J.R. That smile on his lips was somewhat wider, and no longer dreamy but sort of amused. "Is it Tabby?"

He laughed. "No."

She bit her lip so that she didn't ask about other names.

They arrived at her house, and he stopped his dirty truck in front of it. She said, "I can walk across the back. Drive on into your drive."

"I'm doing this right."

"I don't have my front-door key."

"I'll walk you around to the back door. Sit still until I get around and let you out." He stopped half out of his side of the pickup and suggested, "When I get around there, you could unlock your door."

She did that.

He took his time. He moved like any muscled man. He had some pride in his body and knew he was capable of doing just about anything requested of him, and some things nobody required at all. He opened the door widely and then extended his hand for hers. Her hand was very small in his square, rough grip, and her eyes went up his body, seemingly only then realizing how much smaller and different she was from him.

She moved her denim-clad legs around and set her tennies onto the curb. His steady hand was there for her. She rose with seeming effortlessness to stand beside him. "Everyone who has a window facing in this direction is standing by them, watching this."

"If you don't swim, you don't get wet."

He'd said that as if it made good sense, so she was stymied, trying to figure it out as they walked silently down her drive and to her back door. He held out his hand. She shook it, saying, "I had an interesting time. It was different."

"Thank you for going with me. This is our second date, I get a kiss."

"Oh—" Her protest was stopped by his mouth, and being in the "oh" position, her lips were exactly right for receiving his nice, squishy kiss! Her head buzzed and her body tingled, and she became disoriented. But she didn't stagger or fall, because he'd wrapped his arms around her and was holding her crushed against his hard body. The whole episode was simply amazing.

He lifted his mouth and looked down into her eyes. "Did I do that okay?"

She heard an odd-sounding voice croak, "Yes," and turned her swimming head to see who else was there, but they were alone. She'd made that blatantly eager guttural sound?

"Or," he questioned, "should I have done it this way?"

He shifted her body very handily, as if she weighed nothing at all, draped her over his arm, leaned after her and kissed her again, as he ran one hand up her side and over her breast! She choked and murmured, but the kiss was still going on and she couldn't let go of his shoulders for some reason.

There was an offstage crooning sound, and Jan went scarlet to think someone was witnessing her scandalous behavior. Again she found they were alone, and it was she who was giving those sounds of approval.

He stood her on her wobbly legs and said, "Or should I—"

"No!" She backed up, and he followed as if they were dancing, his steps exactly following hers.

"—do this." And he pushed her right against the porch wall and pressed his body into hers as his hands moved up under her arms with the heels of his palms against the sides of her breasts. And he kissed her witless.

After a time, he stepped back and inquired in a perfectly normal voice, "Which would be best for the first kiss?"

Her eyes wouldn't focus, so his image swam in little waves. Her hands flopped around vaguely. Her mouth wanted more. Her body was clamoring for a continuation, an in-depth study. He was a wicked, wicked man. There wasn't anyone who could teach him anything about kissing. The vague shadow of him was poised expectantly. He was waiting for her reply.

What had he asked?

There were just times when a woman gave up the field and didn't try to prove anything at all. Janet said a slurred, "G'night."

But he didn't leave. He tilted his head to one side and said, "Give me your key so I can open your door."

She didn't have a purse. She'd put the key in her pocket. Which one? She patted her body rather vaguely, while he picked up her sweater off the porch floor and held it. She located the key, took it out and looked at it as if she'd never seen it before. When he'd held out his hand, it had been for her key! And she'd just shaken his hand. How betraying. She wasn't that knowledgeable about dating.

He took the key from her palm, opened the screen, unlocked her door and stood back. "Need help undressing?" His tone was all consideration.

She shook her head in something of a wobble. He handed her the sweater. She made it past him and the screen, then through the door. She turned and looked at him.

He chided gently: "You didn't tell me which one was best."

She didn't pretend not to know which what. She reached for the screen door. He did give it up, stepping back. She hooked the screen and mumbled, "All of them." Then she shut the door and shot the bolt, leaning bonelessly against the panel.

She was only aware of herself, until time had passed and she heard him walk carefully across the porch and down the steps. That he had waited, standing by her door, did give her something to think about. Perhaps he hadn't been so indifferent to those torrid kisses as she had thought? What sort of Pandora's box had she been tampering with, here, with this auction?

It had been she who had decided that J.R.'s manners needed to be polished. Well, he surely didn't need any practice in kissing. And she shivered deliciously. But what was he doing kissing her that way, when he'd just told her he had his eye on another woman? Honing skills? He emphatically did not need to do that.

He could get a woman in and out of a car, and he could entertain her in the middle of a whoop-and-holler dance, and he hadn't left her alone or made her follow him around, and he could kiss. Oh, could he kiss! If he could ballroom dance and eat properly, he wouldn't make any woman blush for him.

She needed to see him in clothes.

That sounded very lascivious, as if she'd only seen him ... unclothed. The problem was ... The big stumbling block was ... The crux of the whole thing *now* was that Janet Folger wasn't at all sure she could trust herself alone with him again.

She heard his pickup drive into his driveway. And she listened for a long time before his tread slowly mounted his wooden back steps and crossed his porch. Was he as boggled as she? Why?

They'd grown up together. There was no mystery between them. Nothing.

Bemused, she wandered around getting ready for bed, but she found herself in odd places, doing nothing. Standing at a window, facing J.R.'s silent house. Standing in a doorway, looking at nothing. Standing in the kitchen, not hungry. Staring in the bathroom mirror without seeing herself. She was very distracted.

Jan finally, dreamily, took off her tennies and socks, her top and jeans, then her underwear. And finally she put a silken gown down over her head and settled it on her strangely sensitive body. She never wore a gown. She wore a T-shirt and panties. She absently smoothed her hands over the gown, bemused by the feel of the silk against her skin. Had she ever been aware of that before then?

She crawled onto her bed and pulled the covers up over her alert form ... and she wondered if, next door, J.R. was lying in his own bed?

He was probably flat out, sound asleep and snoring.

Pensively Jan turned over on her side and stared unseeing into the dim space of her bedroom. It was only lust, she reassured herself. Gradually she relaxed, and at last she slept.

He worked Saturday. She did chores and washed clothes and puttered. But he didn't come home all of that day.

She didn't see him on Sunday. Church was a waste of time. She smiled and nodded, but she didn't hear the sermon and she just looked vapid during the hymns.

She had Sunday dinner with Minna and Peggy, and in the afternoon they drove to the lake cottage of friends to swim and see an art film.

On Monday Jan dressed carefully and behaved in a discreet manner, but she was especially kind to everyone who came her way. She was learning how vulnerable humans can be, and the trials put to innocent, unwary bystanders.

Tad had lunch with a whole bunch of women at Dorothy's Do Drop Inn. Jan sat at the next table, and he smiled at her when she spoke to him. He was dressed neatly, his hair was combed nicely and his table manners were perfect. He listened and laughed with the women who were vying for his attention, and Jan wondered if the five hundred would be high enough for her bid.

She couldn't raise her bid unless she sold her car, Tootie, or got a bank loan. She looked at Tad. He'd be worth just about whatever it took. If the five hundred wasn't enough, she'd have to figure another way.

Then Jan found out that Silthy was bidding on Tad, seriously bidding, not just the minimum required of the committee. That Silthy could be serious about bidding for Tad was appalling to Jan. Silthy had resources and gentle determination. How much would she bid? Surely not five hundred dollars. When the minimum bid was four dollars and fifty cents, Silthy wouldn't feel that she had to go clear up to five hundred dollars. Only a fool would bid that much.

Glum, Jan returned to her office and her recalcitrant computer, which was acting so abominably that Jan was convinced computers were of two genders and she'd gotten one of the wrong kind.

In the middle of the afternoon, J.R. treated her to another highway phone-booth call, yelling, "It was my pleasure to escort you on Friday to the Barn, Miss Folger, and I especially appreciated your saying goodnight with such willing cooperation."

She was still gasping indignant breaths, when he yelled in an aside over the traffic sounds whooshing past him, "I'm *coming*!" Then he shouted to her, "—but not satisfactorily."

Jan was shocked. He was really rather crude. That was the second innuendo that he'd perpetrated. No nice woman allowed a man to speak that way without a reprimand. But he hung up. Rude and crude. Junior Busby hadn't changed a bit.

So that night Jan felt compelled to wait for him to get home, so that she could instruct him in gentlemanly conversation, but she went to sleep on his back porch. She and the Witherspoon cat were totally out of it when J.R. came home and found them.

He smiled down on the pair. He picked up the cat by the scruff, lifting it slowly from Jan's lap, and dropped the surprised cat onto the walk where it lashed its tail indignantly.

But J.R. had already forgotten the cat. He sat next to Jan very carefully, not making one sound. Breathing shallowly, he eased Janet onto his furnace lap and spread her over his body. Then he began to take little sipping kisses from her wakening mouth.

She had been dreaming of winning the bid for Tad, so when J.R. kissed her, she thought it was Tad's gratitude. She was amazed that Tad had wanted her to win. She didn't want him to think she wasn't glad that she had, and so she kissed him back. She was quite astonished how practiced Tad was, and how deliciously thrilling it was to be in his arms. She wallowed in being kissed. And his arms were tightly around her while his hands . . . were somewhat shockingly familiar!

She made insincere protesting sounds as her hands crept up his chest and found his shoulders. Then she moved her body in a wiggle that elicited a groan from him. It had a very sexual sound to it, and it made her throat laugh wicked.

He licked a hot tongue in her ear as he whispered, "You're a naughty woman."

She'd never dreamed that Tad would be such a sensual man. What a lovely surprise! He wanted her. Sitting on his lap, even she could know that. She moved her bottom just enough to show that she understood his problem, and she opened her mouth to his seeking tongue, her own tongue questioning his right to invade such a private place.

His tongue stroked hers familiarly and convincingly, so she allowed him entrance. And she shivered and made hungry sounds.

"Why, Janet Folger—" a husky voice breathed hotly "—what are you doing to me?"

To him?

"Let me just unzip this—"

"What?" She was whispering, too.

"I just want to get rid of—"

"No!" Her hushed voice was becoming strident as she asked in shock, "Junior?"

"I thought we'd decided on calling me J.R."

"What are you doing here?" Her whisper was very indignant, and she grasped her dress and pushed at his hands as she tried to get off his lap.

He didn't give up easily. "I'm here on my own back porch. What are you doing, lying sprawled out so temptingly, sleeping on my porch?"

"Your—?" She struggled to get free as she looked around blankly. "What happened to—" But she stopped in time. She remembered where she was and why. She was there to confront J.R. and chide him for being crude.

This was really humiliating. She'd been— She was just about— She couldn't possibly do any lecturing about manners and morals. It was time to retreat. "Let me go."

"Who did you think I was?"

How nasty of him to want to know that. "Let go."

"Whose lap did you think you were wiggling on and what man were you kissing that way?"

"I do beg your pardon. I have no excuse. I was dead tired, and you took me by surprise."

"I did come pretty close, didn't I? But who did you think I was?"

"A dream."

"Why, Janet Folger, do you have hot dreams?"

Blushing painfully, she replied, "Apparently. Please. Let me go."

"You don't know what you've done to me."

She knew.

"Go back to sleep. I'm a patient man."

"No."

"For half an hour. Just doze off and don't pay any attention. I'll wake you up in half an hour, I promise. You need the rest."

"The 'rest' of what?"

And he laughed. "There's hope for you, Jan. You're as human as I. Welcome to the club."

"I must go. Please. I'm embarrassed."

"Why?"

"I . . . am. Don't embarrass me this way."

"Honey, good lust shouldn't embarrass anybody. Just relax and let me show you how nice it could be. Stay awake. Enjoy. Let me just kiss you once more."

"Better not."

"'Not' isn't better."

"You're a very wily man, J.R. Now, let me up."

"I really like having you on my lap. Let's just roll over here and let me be on top for a while."

"I'll yell for Mrs. Witherspoon."

"You wouldn't!"

"Yes."

"She would love that." He promised. "She would poke Mr. Witherspoon and gossip about it and come down and catch us in the very act!"

"He'd have a heart attack. We can't do that to him."

"Let's go inside."

"J.R.," she said with enduring patience. "No. N, O, No."

"You have a wide selfish streak that ought to make you very ashamed of yourself."

She declared: "You have a clever tongue."

"You liked my tongue? Here, let me show you what I can—"

In a hissing whisper, she pretended to yell, "Mrs. Witherspoon."

"You're not only selfish, you're cruel. Here I am as hot as I can get, anxious to play and you want to take your toys and go home. You're a disgrace to woman-kind."

"How often has that kind of talk worked?"

"I just lucked into doing it tonight."

"Lucked?"

"I've never had any opposition before this."

She could believe it. She unwound his arms and was surprised at her hands' reluctance. She sat up on him very carefully. Then she rose awkwardly and took two very cautious steps away from him.

She glanced back at him sprawled so invitingly there, and thought it would be best not to say any-thing more. She ought to get away while she could. If he started again, she wasn't sure what would happen.

He said softly, "Coward."

Four

The next day, the office was dead quiet when J.R. called Jan from the highway phone booth and hollered over the traffic sounds, "Miss Folger, I enjoyed finding you on my porch last night. May I count on you again tonight?"

Jan was appalled. She looked up and saw that it was true. His voice was very loud, and in her office people's heads were turning toward her in surprise as, predictably, J.R. having spoken his requisite piece, hung up.

Jan's boss came from her cubicle and asked, "Problems?"

"No. A friend talking from a phone booth on the highway."

"Short conversation."

"He can't hear me."

"He?" The question came from an interested word selector.

Jan was kind. "A neighbor."

And an excited voice asked, "Junior? He's your neighbor, isn't he?"

"Almost all of his life." Jan's voice was soft.

In a sigh, one voice said, "Some people are so lucky."

But Jan was oddly pensive. Who would live next door to J.R. when Jan married Tad and moved away?

Then just before five, Jan had another call from the highway. J.R. yelled, "I'll meet you at Red Lobster for supper at six-thirty. We've finished a section, and I can get away."

Trying to yell back discreetly, Jan said, "I'm busy—"

But J.R. said, "—can monitor my table manners." And he hung up.

She frowned fruitlessly at the humming phone, and seething, she placed it gently back in its cradle. But she glanced up into the silence of the office to find everyone staring and her boss was again in the doorway of her cubicle.

Jan didn't volunteer anything.

That evening, she met J.R. at the Red Lobster, but he didn't arrive until almost seven. By then, Jan had finished all the crackers in the table basket in order to counter a glass of wine that rested on her empty stomach in a disquieting manner of threatening exuberance. She was relaxed and tolerant. And since she'd paid for the publicity supper and not been reimbursed by this freeloader, she said right away, "We go Dutch."

He raised his eyebrows in surprise and asked, "Really? Why?"

"I can't afford to keep feeding you. All my money is tied up in my bid for Tad."

He barely nodded his head several times. "How much did you bid on me? The rock-bottom minimum? What was that?"

"Four dollars and fifty cents."

"Right."

"I added a penny since you're my neighbor."

He stared in astonishment. "A wild woman. An extra penny!"

"I figured I was safe." She shrugged. "Other women are sure to bid on you, and my bid will be cancelled."

"So it isn't all contributions? If someone bids higher for Tad, your granny's money is safe in the bank?"

"Yes."

"Only the top bidders have to pay." He clarified that.

"The base bids are to guarantee we'll have something to give the park department for the trees."

He figured it. "Twenty-two and a half dollars all totaled? Each winner pays?"

"Well, we all know Tad is going to bring in a nice amount."

"Women are fathomless. Why would anyone want Tad?"

She explained. "He's charming. Courteous. Clean. Neat. He smiles and is glad to see people."

"Sounds like a house dog. You haven't mentioned that I've showered and worn a suit, shirt and tie."

She smiled. "Shoes and socks."

"I shaved."

"You'll do very well. You really look nice."

"So do you." He could then study her body. She was wearing a sweater vest that matched her green skirt. Her starched shirt was white with green stripes and the open neckline gaped just a bit, so he glimpsed the elusive chain again. What was on that chain? Women wore chains to display something. A Girl Scout medal? A gold heart with pictures of her parents? What did she leave concealed from the world? He'd never seen the bottom of that chain. Why didn't she pull it out from between her round breasts—

He couldn't be thinking about her body or he'd forget to eat, carry her out of there to his truck and drag her into the bushes somewhere, so that he could pull that chain out and see what was on it.

Why didn't he just ask? Simple. Just say, "What are you hiding down there in the warm, soft place where your sweet breasts push together and drive me crazy?" Well, of course he couldn't say that, but he could say, "What's on that chain?" He didn't want her to tell him. He wanted to find out on his own.

To find out, he'd have to get really familiar with her, and he was working on that. See? He wasn't a lecher, he was an investigator. A solver of puzzles.

He smiled at her, sitting to his left at the four-seat table. Tonight, he was going to charm the pants off her. She'd change her bid to him, and they'd celebrate during the entire festival. It would be something she'd remember all her life.

He told her, "Order what you like. This is on me."

"Thank you, but no. This isn't a date. We go Dutch. I'm doing this for a neighbor and ultimately for my club. Anyway, I'm not very hungry. I ate all the crackers while I waited for you to show up."

"I could have been here on time, but I'd have been coming right off the job, and I'd have had to sit outside. They wouldn't have allowed me in here."

"There are other men here who aren't in suits."

"They've showered."

Her eyes twinkled. "Oh."

He ordered for them and ordered another glass of wine for her. He had beer. He relished his first drink of the cold brew. "Ah." His pleasure made her smile. He told her, "You have pretty eyes."

"So are yours." She told him that earnestly as she looked into his.

"Do you like anything else about me?" he encouraged and smiled confidently.

"You don't tell secrets."

"I could be selective in who I tell secrets to."

"Then you do?"

"Not the ones that matter."

"Do you like working outside? Would you like better summer hours? You've worked so hard since you came back to Byford that no one has seen you. I haven't seen you at all. Hardly."

"I thought I had more time."

"More time?"

"I didn't realize you'd talk me into being in the auction."

"Oh." But she frowned a little. Had she talked him into it? She thought she'd just asked—oh, yes. Her busy tongue had gone right on and coaxed him. "Don't you want to be auctioned?"

"It makes me uncomfortable to think of having to spend time with some fool woman who would pay money to be with me."

"I should think that would flatter you."

"I don't think you look at women the way I do."

"That doesn't particularly surprise me. I probably can guess . . . how you look at women."

He smiled. "You think you can?"

"Of course."

"How." It wasn't a question, but an encouragement for her to talk to him.

"I . . . don't believe I should get involved in this discussion."

"Why not?"

"I'm a woman."

"I had noticed. But Peter confirmed that to me some years ago."

"How tacky of him."

J.R. smiled at her. "How do you think I look at women?"

"As females."

"Well, sure. Don't you look at men as males?"

She moved her head in a series of needless tilts that showed she was well-bred and therefore not approving of this conversation, but that she was open-minded enough to participate. "I look at men as people."

"Ah." He smiled at her and tapped his beer bottle to her almost full wineglass. "To people."

She lifted the glass and sipped, but she was silent.

"Define 'people.'"

Jan gave him an off-putting look and replied, "'People' are a body of people living in one country, under one government. But I think of people as a gathering of persons who are human with all the thoughts and hopes and ideals that unite us on this planet."

"Wow. And I'm supposed to think all that when I see a . . . woman?"

"You asked how I thought you see women. I don't believe you see them as people who share ideas and hopes. I think you see a female body."

He considered that as if it was a new idea and then said, "Yeah. Basically, that's about it. I notice her face, then the part that holds that off the ground, so that would include her neck and the portion between there and her legs. That would make up part of the body, I suppose."

"But not her clothes?"

"That would probably be next."

"So up until then, she's naked?"

"I might notice if she's hostile or friendly. Or if she's pregnant. That generally indicates a woman is taken."

Jan sighed—pointedly—then she tightened the corners of her mouth and looked across the other tables to the wall.

"This is an interesting discussion," J.R. said cheerfully. "I wonder if other guys ever analyzed how they look at women. I may take a poll. If I do this, can I get credits?"

"From what?"

"You. If I can find men who look on women as people, will you be interested in the score?"

"How are you going to word the questions?"

"Singular. Question: 'When you look at a woman, what do you see?' I'll clean up the gross ones."

They were being served and their waiter asked carefully, "Clean up . . . what?"

J.R. looked up kindly and said, "Language."

"Oh." And he left them to their meal.

J.R. was starved and ate with concentration. He'd been at it some time before she realized he could eat perfectly well. That made her a little sad. He could dress and eat, he was clean and orderly, he knew how to get a woman in and out of a car, he could kiss.... God, could he kiss. And he could dance—he didn't dance at all. "Your table manners would make your mother proud of you."

J.R. looked up blankly and blinked once, then he realized what she'd been monitoring and said, "Oh," as if he'd failed in some strange way and was disappointed. "I slurp with soup."

"I doubt soup would be served at the dinner."

"You haven't seen me eat anything but fish."

"J.R., you do very well. You won't make any partner uncomfortable. I don't have any criticism of you, at all. You will be excellent."

He looked stony.

"However..."

His stare snapped up to hers. "What."

"The only dancing I've witnessed was none at all. You just stood there and hugged me."

He put down his fork and sighed in defeat. "So, you know."

"You like hugging women?"

"Well...yes, but I can't dance."

She became efficient. "There isn't much time."

"I have very good rhythm," he assured her. "And I can vary it." He smiled guilelessly.

She looked at him quickly and just saw his earnest, willing expression. "I'll do what I can."

To show helpful cooperation he offered, "I have some great tapes and a boom box."

"It's too bad Byford doesn't have a dance studio for professional instruction."

"I think so, too, but you're very kind to want to help me out."

"You're my neighbor." She gently moved one hand briefly to indicate it was nothing. But then she found herself saying tersely, "Of course, when I was *desperate* for a partner in the eighth grade, you refused to go."

"God, Jan, I was *seventeen*! How can a guy who is *seventeen* go to an eighth-grade dance? It would have ruined my reputation."

"If it hadn't been for Freddy, I'd have just died."

"The hero." It was a sour labeling.

She agreed, "His mother made him. My mother asked his mother. It was one of the worst evenings in my life."

"You're kidding! Something like that left such an impression? Where are your priorities? Is that why Parson...? You know, Jan, you are critical of how men look on women, then you admit, at your age, that something that happened at a school dance when you were fourteen years old branded you all this time. Now that's..." He scrambled over several very poor word choices and came limping up verbally with, "...strange."

"It was important then."

"But it's *still* important to you. What if you don't win Tad? Is that going to turn you into a recluse?"

"No one will know what I bid."

"Three women will."

"There you go again, casting stones on 'women!'" Her feathers were ruffled, and she twitched in her chair as she allowed her fork to play with her fish. "Anyway, I doubt if anyone else would be foolish enough...uh...would bid that much on Tad. No one has ever gone that high before this."

"Foolish? Did you hear the word you used? You *admit* that bidding that much is foolish, and you're pitching your grandmother's hard-saved money out on...Tad?"

"It's going for trees!" she spoke through tightened lips and clenched teeth.

"And if you win, you get the dog."

She sat up very straight, put her knife and fork precisely across the center of her plate to indicate she was through with this meal, and then put her hands in her lap. She lifted her chin and stared off somewhat to her left so that he was out of her line of vision. She was furious.

"We're quarreling," he said, as if they'd reached a goal.

Enunciating perfectly, she replied, "We have seldom had a civil word in all our lives."

"That isn't true, at all. You were very difficult to fight with, all our lives. You either flounced away, or started screaming, 'Mrs. Busby!' and Mother would come out on the porch and yell, 'Jun-ior! You be nice!'" He imitated his mother's call and command just perfectly.

Jan ducked her head, but he'd seen her quick smile. "Your mother is a sweet lady."

"She thought you were perfect. You notice she never asked what had happened, she just told *me* to 'be nice' to you. She never knew what a rotten little kid you were. You were always interfering and never cooperating, and we always had to do everything your way.''

"Of course," she agreed.

"Mother loves you."

"I miss her."

He suggested. "You ought to go see them. They'd like that."

"There's never time enough. Vacations, I go out to see my folks and my sisters. I miss them all. I always thought they'd all stay here."

"Families move around a lot." He gestured to indicate that. "That's why we're here in this country. The whole population is made up of wanderers who came to this country to see what it would be like. To be independent. To be free. We're the descendants of restless peoples. What do you suppose we're all looking for, that we have to keep moving on? It's no surprise that we were the first to the moon."

"Other people's families stay around Byford, why did ours all leave?"

"You stayed. I came back." He looked at her.

"You're gone all the time. I've hardly seen you since you came back." It occurred to her she'd said several betraying times that, since he'd returned, she hadn't been able to see him enough. She looked at her hands.

"I've been working my...self ragged this year." He assured her. "I need a nest egg, so that I can start up my own business. I want to start a repair business for people who haven't the time or the interest or the skill to do small repairs, like appliances. Or cleaning. Not a maid service, but hard cleaning—walls, garages, attics. That way, there aren't any emergency calls, nights and weekends, just hard work."

She nodded. "I have a door that doesn't close. One corner needs to be planed a little."

His head bobbed a couple of times in agreement. "This is an aging town that's going to become static. Enough business for a living but nothing spectacular. Enough money to take care of things. A good solid life."

"But the young people will leave."

He replied, "Some will. But Sam and Betsy came back. So did Warren and Phoebe. This is a great town. It's a good place for kids. There are enough people to be abrasive and keep things stirred up. There are good parks. Good people who are civic-minded. Solid farms around. This is a perfect town."

She added: "We got rid of the massage parlors."

"Well, darn."

"I knew it!"

He looked surprised. "I work in construction! Do you know how knotted up my muscles can get? I could use a good massage."

Her eyelids fluttered a little as her glance went just to his shoulders. An odd feeling shivered in the pit of her stomach at the very thought of having him naked on her kitchen table and rubbing his tired muscles....

"—you like some—Janet?"

"Hmm?" She turned large-pupiled eyes to him.

And he was stunned as he stared. What had she been thinking?

Jan asked, "What did you say?"

Distracted, he replied, "He wants to know if we'd like something for dessert."

She smiled gently at the waiter. "Vanilla ice cream. No. Lemon sherbet. No. Crème de menthe."

"We don't have any."

She was disappointed. "Oh, well."

His eyes still on her bemused face, J.R. said, "We'll find some."

"There's no need—"

"Oh, yes." He turned to the waiter. "The meal was delicious."

The waiter looked at Janet's almost untouched plate in a speaking way.

"I had too many crackers," she apologized.

The waiter discreetly laid the bill face-down halfway between the couple and left. J.R. took the bill and put the tip under the edge of his plate, then reached out a hand to pull back Janet's chair as she left the table independently, and he stood up. He ushered her out very nicely, paid the cashier and took her out to his pickup. "We'll come get your car later."

"No. I need to get home. I have to work tomorrow."

The first drop of rain hit. J.R. opened out his arms and said to the sky, "Please, God."

"You want it to rain? We've had enough this year. You ought not ask God for rain when we don't need it."

"Construction people don't work in a good hard rain."

She exclaimed, "So *that's* why we have floods!"

"Hadn't you realized that?"

"And your pickup gets something of a wash."

"My truck embarrasses you." He looked at her, waiting.

"Not really."

"You resist me." He said that as a revelation to her.

"Resist you?"

"You've always been crazy about me, but you resist admitting it."

She laughed heartily, trying to stop and going on laughing.

He watched, smiling. "You know that's the truth."

She went into another peal of laughter. Her eyes held dancing lights in the late summer dusk and she looked at him to share his joke. He was smiling slightly. She acknowledged: "You're so funny. You know full well that's just silly. You've always teased me. You were really very irritating."

He countered. "You were prissy."

"I've never been that."

"You are now."

"I am not," she exclaimed indignantly. "I am mature. I don't stoop to make others look silly or ridiculous. It's unkind."

"Did you think I wanted you to look silly? I was only trying to get your attention."

She protested, "Oh, for Pete's sake."

"Him, again." J.R. lifted his hands out and let them flop back to his sides.

"Who?"

"Your partner in playing doctor."

She put out her arms in a very free way and said, "There you go again."

"I was jealous."

She laughed. "I enjoyed dinner with you. Your manners are better than mine."

"I've always been perfect."

She shook her head. "Don't push it." She gestured to the building holding the restaurant. "This has been very nice." She opened her car door. "You do need to practice dance steps. You can't just stand around and hug women. You have to move your feet."

"I don't mind doing it my way."

"What a lecher." She got into her car.

He closed her door. "I'll call you tomorrow—"

"That's another thing. You call, and there's all that noise and you can't hear me."

"You hear me." Then, as she had, he indicated the building. "You did come to have supper with me."

"I didn't know how to reach you to tell you that I couldn't."

"But you could. You did come here."

"Yes." She looked up at him. "Thank you for a pleasant evening. Good night."

"I'll follow you home."

She grinned. "You live next door."

There were several things he could have said, but he waited too long. She started the motor, gave him another glance, then backed her car from the slot, turned and left the lot.

He felt another drop of rain and saw that the dust on the top of his truck was splatted with drops. He looked up at the sky. Then he got into the pickup and went home.

He drove his truck onto the grass in his backyard as Jan was closing and locking her garage.

He got out and went over to her. "Miss Folger, I enjoyed our date tonight."

"It wasn't a date."

"I paid."

"Yes, but I told you not to do that. It was only to see if you knew how to handle yourself. I'd never realized your mother had taught you so much."

"You thought I was a slob?"

"Well . . ." She really had no reply.

"You're supposed to kiss me good-night. You can't eat a meal at my expense and not give up a kiss."

"Of course I can."

"It's a rule."

She retorted. "I had dinner with Judge Collins and I didn't kiss him."

"That's different."

"One doesn't kiss neighbors." She said that with conviction. "I paid for the light supper we had before the publicity pictures for the auction, and you've paid me back with a meal. We're even."

"I need the practice."

She laughed. "Go home. It's raining." And she ran for her porch.

So he jogged over to his own porch and looked out at his truck. Then he went inside and changed into cutoffs. He gathered the equipment of cleaner and bucket, sponge and old towels before going out to wash his pickup in the rain.

From her window, Jan watched. Then she put on scruffies and went out with her own bucket and sponge. She explained, "Beautifying the neighborhood." And she helped him.

He handed her the squirt bottle of soap and commented, "You've always been a picky woman."

The warm rain pelted down and they were thoroughly soaked. He turned the hose on her, and she threw a soggy sponge at him. He caught it handily, then started after her and she squealed and ran.

They played dodge 'em. And she did a good show of courage and rashness, giving as good as she got. She stumbled over the bucket and said, "King's X!" until she had staggered free, put the bucket formally on the porch steps and fled.

She got the hose and aimed the water at his head, but he ducked under the spray and tackled her. She was like an eel, squirming and slithering, and they laughed themselves helpless.

Panting, they finally called a truce. And they sat in the wet grass in the rain, and they struggled to catch their breath. He told her she looked like a drowned cat.

And she replied, "Always the flatterer."

Then he said, "You're gorgeous."

And she laughed in disbelief.

"Did you hurt yourself on the bucket?"

"They'll probably have to do surgery tomorrow."

"Let me see."

"How can you see in this mess?"

He moved to his hands and knees and crawled to her.

She blinked in surprise. He seemed so primal like that. His shape loomed in the rain. His skin glistened in the lights and shadows of his body. He was thrilling to see. And a little intimidating. J.R.?

She didn't move, and he took her ankle into his big hand. "Where did you hurt it?"

"It's fine."

"Show me."

"It's nothing." She protested. "Really."

"Where does it hurt? I saw you limp."

"Right there."

He put his big, hard hand gently on her shin and moved it over it so lightly, feeling. "I don't feel broken skin."

"I told you that."

"You'll probably bruise. You were always bat-
tered. You're so reckless."

She declared, "I'm tough."

"Yeah."

Then he put his head down and kissed her shin.

All sorts of things happened inside her body. It was
what erotica was all about. Jan knew now what was
meant by that word. She was owl-eyed with the
knowledge.

Five

J.R. turned off the hose and stood with Jan in the warm downpour to inspect the miraculous transformation of his truck into a recognizable color. Jan said in satisfaction, "I'd wondered what color it was, but I'd never have guessed it was green."

"What color did you think it was?"

"Silver. All hero vehicles in books are silver."

He said cautiously, "I don't believe I've ever seen a silver pickup, but I'll paint it."

"I like green."

He agreed quickly, "I'll leave it green."

She smiled up at him. "I enjoyed the romp in the rain. Good night."

He said, "I have crème de menthe in the house. Come in and have a sip or two."

"Why...all right. But I'm dripping wet."

"I have a tile floor, and we'll stay in the kitchen. I need a better look at your shin."

She hesitated, remembering fantasizing about having him naked on her kitchen table for a massage. His very mention of the word "kitchen" was erotic to her. "Well . . . all right. I'd enjoy a little sip."

"And I have dry towels."

She grinned.

So he had lured her into his house. If he was very careful and did everything just right, maybe he could lure her into his bed . . . to warm her. He was sure as hell hot enough to do that all right.

They dripped up onto his porch and stood for a minute, hand-stripping water from their arms and hair. She wrung the tail of her T-shirt, and he squeezed the water from one of the towels not needed on the car but soaked by the rain.

J.R. was already barefoot, and Jan removed her tennies. He waited as she did that.

He gave the damp towel to her and watched as she soaked some of the rain from her water-bedraggled darkened hair, before running the wrung towel over her arms and legs. He then used it to wipe down his chest and legs. They laughed at each other in the marvelous freedom they'd shared.

She wondered if Tad would have played that way in the rain. He went along with the crowd. He probably would have, if everyone else had. But if she had thrown the sponge at Tad, he probably would just have laughed and not chased and teased her, as J.R. had done just then.

That was probably because Tad had never *had* to chase a woman. Unlike the dearth of females around J.R., there had always been so many vying for Tad's attention that Tad had never needed to know how to tease a woman into noticing him.

So J.R. had had to learn the clever ways that men had invented to call female attention to themselves. And he was innovative enough that he could seize whatever opportunity that came along...like playing in the rain.

Jan looked at J.R. And in that stunning minute, she realized there would be women who would find him attractive. He was attractive. Half-naked and wet, he was excessively male. She ought not go into his house with him.

He opened the door and stood aside for her, and she...went inside.

J.R. came in after her. She turned at bay and stared at him. She was embarrassed to be there.

He disappeared into the half bath at the bottom of the stairs and reappeared with a stack of towels. There was a wide variety of designs and colors. The towels were probably cast-offs from his mother's linen closet.

J.R. lifted Jan up to sit on the counter, and he carefully examined the red mark left by her encounter with the bucket. There wasn't any way at all that he could elaborate the hurt. So he kissed it again. "I made it well. Anything else you need cured?"

She shook her head and slid off the counter.

He grinned at Jan, sorting out and handing her a green towel. "Your cheeks are all pink from running around in the rain." Then he frowned at her. "Or are you feverish? You haven't caught a chill, have you?"

Even as she shook her head in denial, he took the premise of her being chilled as an excuse to crowd close into her space and put his hand on her forehead. And since she shrank away, his other hand captured her shoulder to hold her where he wanted her. Then he had the audacity to lean over and kiss her forehead.

His mouth burned her skin. That ought to convince him that there was nothing wr—

But he said, "My hand cooled your forehead. I have to feel your throat." And his big left hand moved from her shoulder to the nape of her neck and the opposite hand helped to enclose her entire neck like a too-wide slave collar.

Beneath his little finger at the nape of her neck, he felt that chain. And he looked down to see it angling down between her breasts beneath the wet T-shirt. On her nape, his little finger wiggled under her neck band and under that chain, and his finger tugged. The chain tightened, and in front it pulled a little taut under the wet cotton cloth. Whatever was hung from that chain was tightly held between her breasts.

She lifted her camel eyelashes to look into his hazel eyes. "I'd better go on home."

He told her, "Your spider-leg eyelashes are clumped together with the rain."

He could have been indulging in his usual teasing, but his eyes were serious. His hands scorched her, and his ears pointed. Her wide-pupiled eyes stared up at him. "Your ears are pointed."

"I'm kin to Mr. Spock."

"Oh." She accepted that, so it was a good indication of her state. She added, "As you can see, I am quite cool."

"You're probably having chills."

"No—"

"Let me get you a slug of whiskey."

She protested: "Good heavens, no!"

"Just the crème de menthe?"

"A very little bit. I must go home. I have a great deal to do tomorrow."

"What?"

"I have to go to work, of course, and in the afternoon I must see about . . . some business."

"Office or personal?" he wanted to know.

"Personal."

"Anything I can help with?"

"Oh, no. Thank you, but no."

He turned and looked at her in a different, serious way. "You know you could count on me in any problem you might have. You would only have to tell me what you need."

"Why . . . thank you, Junior." She was so touched. He'd been so earnest.

He studied her a minute more, their gazes locked, then he went to a cabinet and removed a variety of bottles holding various levels of liquids. He found the squat bottle he wanted, and opened another cabinet. He had several of the little glasses that had once held prepackaged shrimp cocktails. He poured the green liqueur into two of those and handed her one.

He lifted his glass, considered and said, "To dreams."

She smiled at his charming fantasy and lifted her own glass. They took the tasting sip, and it was just right to follow the fish dinner. She asked, "What is your dream?"

"That everything goes my way." He gestured, openhanded, to show that such a thing was only as it should be.

"That isn't a dream, that's ambition."

"It's the same thing."

"No." She shook her head a couple of times. "Dreams are gossamer webs of imagination and trust. Ambition is using one's skills."

"That's an interesting view."

"What is yours?" she inquired.

"That things go the way I want them."

"For your new business?"

"That, too."

"What else?" she probed.

"My life."

"Are you glad you've come back to Byford?"

"I'll see."

She gasped. "You might not stay?"

"It depends."

She was feeling frustrated by his evasions and urged, "On what?"

"My way."

"So we're back to ambition. I thought you didn't want too much, just hard work and enough money."

"That still holds." He watched her.

"Then what is the pivotal part?"

"The dream."

She finally asked it: "The ... woman you want?"

"Yeah."

"Oh."

"What's your dream, Petunia?"

She shrugged. "I just take life as it comes. I haven't an overview of the years." She looked to the side and studied his stove. "I suppose I really ought to have a plan. Maybe that's why I put Grandmother's money on Tad."

"So," he said softly, "you aren't just giving money for trees, you're plotting on snaring ... Tad?"

How could he put such distaste into just saying "Tad?" That had to be a talent. "In spite of your opinion, there isn't anything wrong with Tad. He's a nice man."

"Nice." He tasted the word through his teeth, with a squinched-up face. "Promise you'll never call me nice."

"You aren't, so you don't have to worry about that. The first time that you said my eyelashes were like spider legs, I went home and mother stopped me from cutting them off. My sisters laughed and said you had a *crush* on me! Can you believe that?"

"Yeah."

"Sure you do. I've never seen anyone who taunted and annoyed and irritated as deliberately as you did."

"That was before I got élan. I've got real class now. I can charm a woman right out of her pants."

"You're only vulgar."

"Me?" He put his hand to his chest. "I? You jest."

"What other man would chase a woman around the backyard in the rain and hit her with a soggy sponge?"

"You loved it."

She grinned. "It was fun. I haven't played that way in years."

"Remember the cave?"

"That was just wonderful. We were lucky no one was in it when it collapsed. I've read since of kids..."

"We had a great growing-up time. It was special. Your imagination made it that way."

"No." She shook her head with the word. "I just went along cautiously. It was you who was the adventurer. But you always made me test things out, so you knew whether it was safe for you. Like smoking that cigar."

He refilled her small glass almost to the brim. "You convinced me, that day, never to smoke. God, you were sick. But you have to remember that while I had the ideas, you couldn't stand to have anyone else be the adventurer. It was you who insisted on going first. Remember when you got tangled up in the chains at the sawmill?"

"And you left me there." She tacked on the accusation.

"I went for help!"

"I was grounded for two weeks."

"But we had the can phones."

She looked at him. "It was nice growing up with you."

"I'm still nice."

She smiled a tiny bit. "So you admit being nice is okay?"

"Oh, hell."

She looked at J.R. fondly. Her memories made her smile tenderly.

He came closer, set his empty glass on the counter behind her and said huskily, "I have other talents you ought to sample before you go roaring off into your 'Tad adventure,' riding on your grandmother's money."

"What sorts of talents?"

He smiled. "Like kissing. I've honed that skill quite a bit since you first tried to teach me how."

"You were so indifferent."

"I'd been threatened, at home, to guard you with my life," he explained.

"Your mother is precious."

"Maybe she is to you, but she's a hard-nosed feminist and tried to stuff me into a box, limiting me to being equal to a woman."

"Oh?" she questioned.

"Let's erase that last. You have no idea how I got drilled with the responsibility of taking care of you, seeing to it that no other male harmed you, besides leaving you alone and not experimenting with you, and *then* you wanted to learn to kiss!"

"I already knew how," she sassed. "Remember Peter."

"I hit him where it didn't show."

"Did you really?"

"He told me about playing doctor with you, and I told him he wasn't to tell anyone else, never to do it again, and I hit him. Why did you pick him of all people? That twerp."

In an irritated way she retorted, "Well, you wouldn't."

He gave her a long, long, smoking look and said in a reedy voice, "Why don't you ask me, now?"

At the edge of her vision, Jan noted that the lascivious kitchen table had started pulsating. A very strange tingling went over her, into her body, oddly, and her heart shivered and forgot how it was supposed to function. She became a little faint. "I . . ."

"You're afraid of me because you know that I want you."

"Now, J.R.—"

"You think Tad is safe. That he isn't physical. But he *is* male. He would want to have sex. He'd be inept, but he would try."

"Inept?"

"He'd fumble it and turn you off sex forever, and you'd miss knowing it and me." He took a step nearer, and she could hear his breathing. The sound was different from anything she'd ever experienced. His *breathing?* Everybody breathed...but the sound seemed to fix her failing heartbeat because it picked up. Then it began thundering along strangely, and she wobbled.

His big, strong hands moved to her and took hold of her waist, and she was against the heat of his hard body, with his bare, hairy chest and his head bent down in very slow motion. But she did manage to make her mouth meet his in an impossible maneuver that entailed lifting her immobile chin just a fraction.

And he kissed her.

Before her mind went fuzzy with sensations, she knew this was a different kiss. She already knew he was skilled, but this was the epitome. *This* was what the poets meant.

She could feel his heart thundering away as if he'd run a hundred miles. And knowing she did that to him made her insides quiver in marvelous ways that were thrilling. There were excitations shivering around in interesting places. Her breasts pushed against her bra outrageously, and her mouth opened and their tongues touched. Lightning struck down in a soul-splitting charge that jarred the entire room.

She clung to him helplessly, her mouth glued to his, her hands restless on his shoulders and head, her body trying to meld with his. She realized he had her bottom against the wicked table that was helping her body to be closer to his. How kind of him.

She began making little noises and felt him pulling her wet T-shirt up and sliding his burning hands on her bare, cool skin. He bunched the cloth and pulled it up and *he took it off her!* He'd leaned back to look down her chest, and she realized she was half-naked. For Janet Folger, that was shocking.

He neglected to notice that she was shocked. He was reaching for that chain that slid down between her breasts. He put his fingers up to lift the chain, and she grabbed for her bra and held on, saying, "No. There you go again. My word! You're like an octopus. I thought by now you'd have settled down a little."

"Well, you let Peter."

"He was harmless."

"I'm not?"

She knew he wasn't. She shook her head.

His voice raspy, he questioned, "Did you think I was after your goodies?"

She knew the most erotic sweep of sensual shivers she'd ever encountered. How astonishing. She peeked at J.R. and again noted peripherally that the sexually unbridled table was shimmering eagerly off to the side of her vision. What would it be like to push J.R. over on that table and...massage him? She murmured, "I have to go home."

He kept himself immobile, waiting to see if she meant it.

So if she didn't move to leave, he would know that she was inviting all *kinds* of things. Like... She'd best go right now. Now. But nothing worked. Her body stayed there, her foot didn't move. She struggled inside her inert body and looked pitifully up into his avid eyes. "Help me move."

Was that pitiful little voice . . . hers? Surely not. She was stern. One hand flopped. She took a deep breath and saw that he watched her chest do that. She looked down and saw her lace bra was not much better than nothing at all.

She looked back up at J.R. and his mouth was smiling just a bit. He thought she was going to stay? She exerted tremendous determination and straightened her back. He liked that. But she turned and took a step to go around him, and he frowned.

Since she could get one step done, the next came dragging, but she did take the second step. She looked at him pleadingly. "Open the door."

He didn't move.

If she had to stop and actually open the door, she might lose momentum and give up. She asked, "Please?"

He looked down and his shoulders slumped in defeat. That made her feel bad. Her eyes took on an expression of sympathy without her brain's permission, and her lips parted. The Great Escape would have all been over right then, but he was controlling himself and he didn't glance back at her to see her faltering resolve.

He went over and reluctantly opened the door, but he stood beside it and watched her slow approach. "You don't have to be so careful. I'm not going to jump you."

"You are stunningly stupid."

"Stupid?" He frowned. "What do you mean?"

"When you're more mature, I'll tell you." Her inner self struggled heroinely and she made it through the door, across the porch, down the steps and into the cooling warm rain. She sloshed over into her own yard and into her own house, safe at last. Damn.

She dragged her body up the stairs and into the bathroom. She reached to remove her T-shirt and realized she'd left it over at J.R.'s house. And she looked into the mirror. Good grief! She was a horror! How had J.R. ever gotten up the nerve to actually kiss her? He was desperate. That could be the only excuse for kissing a female who looked the way she did. She shuddered.

By rote she showered, blow-dried her hair, pulled on another, drier cotton T-shirt and panties and went to bed, to sleep, perchance to dream?

Ah, and she did dream.

Erotica. Technicolor and stereophonic sound. His body hotly wet with strong muscles moving under bronzed flesh. Hers sliding under his. His breathing broken, their mouths squeaking and popping. The sounds of their groping, rubbing hands. Moans and gasps.

But...the dream never came to climax. He'd get up and say it was time for him to get to work. Or she would be distracted by whether they were in his bed or hers, as if that actually mattered. And she'd suddenly wonder if she had changed the sheets and which ones were on the bed. Who cared?

Something always interfered. Or J.R. turned into Tad, who questioned what on earth they were doing? And she was so startled. She couldn't figure out what had happened to J.R., and she floundered in her explanations to Tad while she tried to locate her clothing as she noticed that everyone else was there, clothed, and looking at her very oddly.

Jan wakened grumpily to blasting sunshine that irritated the liver out of her. She clumped around, getting her body fed and dressed for work. She drove there and everyone was discussing the terrific lightning bolt that split a big oak out by Jan's house!

"It did?" she was puzzled.

"You mean you *didn't* hear it? I was blocks from you and it about had me on the ceiling with my fingernails and toenails holding me up there!"

Then Jan recalled the feeling when J.R. had kissed her and she had felt the flash of heavenly light and the house had quaked. It hadn't been his kiss?

She left the exclaiming group and moved like a zombie. She then fought with her stupid computer all morning, mostly winning. Just because she'd found out that she loved J.R., did that make her computer jealous?

In a stillness that generally indicated that an earthquake was coming, she blinked several times. My God, she thought appalled, I love J.R.? Surely not. And she examined her heart as her head kept saying, "Surely not," in its empty cavern of echoes that were most annoying.

Specific parts of her quarreled with her head for leaving J.R. and his gorgeous body over there all alone last night, when he'd made it perfectly clear that she'd have been welcome to stay. That was sex. Her body sighed in a swooning way, and its yearning punished Jan.

So. He had a great body.

And playing in the rain had been fun. They'd known each other all their lives, just about. Why had she never felt this way before now?

She'd needed to see something of the world before committing herself to being a wife and mother. She wanted his children.

He probably only wanted to play around. It still irked him that she had played doctor with Peter but not with him. She stretched in her chair, discreetly, and lifted her feet to straighten out her legs. Then she relaxed and propped an elbow on her desk in order to use that hand to prop up her chin. She felt dreamy.

He was competitive. He wanted to do what Peter had when she was six. He wanted to look at her. What else would he want to do? And she smiled. When he played doctor, he probably would just want to give her injections.

Peter had cried because he'd had those growths that she didn't have, but she'd thought his growths were fascinating. In all probability, he'd adjusted to the flaws. His wife was pregnant again.

Jan thought about J.R. getting her pregnant. She became vapid and unresponsive, thinking of that, so Peggy had to shake Jan's shoulder and ask, "What are you thinking about?"

"Hmm?" Jan asked formally, raising her eyebrows.

"Everyone has left for lunch. Aren't you going?"

"Yes," Jan replied. She got her purse and stood up. "Coming?"

Peggy said, "I've been."

And Jan looked at the clock. Almost twelve-thirty? Good gravy. She exited with all the dignity she could muster. Being in love made a woman rather unreliable. Missing lunch?

She decided not to go to Dorothy's Do Drop Inn; she'd have to explain being late. What woman would admit to daydreaming about Junior getting her pregnant?

Then she thought about her bid on Tad. That did rankle J.R. The idea of causing J.R. to be disturbed did marvelous things to Jan. But she needed to switch her bid on Tad to J.R. She'd just go on letting J.R.

think she was bidding on Tad, and she'd be surprised when she found that she'd won—ta-dah—J.R. And she might pretend to be disgruntled.

She walked with more of a stride. She smiled at nothing. She ignored greetings, as if they hadn't been called to her, because her attention was occupied on joggling J.R. She thought she just might wait for him tonight on his back porch.

She looked up at the bright sky. Who would ever have thought that such a day could come after that heavy rain last night?

And she remembered running and playing in the warm, rain-drenched darkness . . . with J.R. Then she remembered his shattering kiss. And she laughed aloud when she thought that the sound and house trembles were caused by lightning striking a tree, and she'd accepted that it had all been from J.R.'s kiss.

J.R.'s kiss. Would it be as remarkable without the cosmic help of a lightning bolt? She'd have to see. Yes. She certainly would.

Six

Jan went to see one of the bid-trio committee, Carol Meeks, at her office and said, "Uh, Carol, I would like to change my bid."

"No."

Jan was shocked. "What do you mean, 'no?' It's my money. I can bid any way I want to."

"All bids are final. Look at your receipt. If we started allowing people to change their minds, we'd go wild trying to keep track. You bid on Tad, and that's it." Then she looked up at Jan and her face changed. "Who do you want to bid on?"

"I thought you just said all the bids were final?"

"They are. You can bid on anyone you like. It's the highest bid that counts. You can bid on another of the five but you'll have to go higher than the five hundred."

Jan looked around in jerks and said, "Hush!"

"You know what you bid, and so do we."

"'We?'"

Carol was very patient. "The committee of three."

"If I have changed my mind, couldn't the three of you allow me to change my bid?"

"No. All bids—"

"—are final."

Craftily Carol asked with slow, thoughtful words, "If...we *would* allow you to change...your bid, who would you bid on?"

"I'll have to see."

"This isn't a be-all and end-all auction. It's only for a weekend date, but it's primarily to raise money for trees."

Jan gave her a very carefully neutral look and said, "Yes."

"If you want to bet...uh...bid on another of the five, you need to get it done. Time is fleeting. There's only one week left until the auction dinner."

"I know." Jan flared her eyes. Then she slowly turned and started away without another word. Carol called. "See you at the dinner on Wednesday next week."

Jan looked back briefly, as if to verify that such a person existed, before she went on out of the office and exited the building without remembering how she had accomplished that.

She found herself on the street, undecided which way she'd go. She was stuck with Tad. She would have to endure his company all of the festival weekend. Who would be with J.R.? What was she to do? Lord, how had she gotten herself into this fix? Why hadn't she known the real J.R.? She'd grown up with him! She ought to have remembered the few times that he'd been sick, and how dull life had been. And when he left Byford, that had been such a tear when he'd gone away to IU. And then his family had left and the Sniders had moved in. Then *her* family had moved to Colorado. She'd completely forgotten what it was like to be with Junior.

How could she have forgotten?

She'd walked too far. She turned around and began to trudge back to her office. Then she found a public phone, called in and said she had been seized with a horrendous headache and she couldn't come back that afternoon. Peggy was so concerned that Jan got a real headache and knew it had been lurking in her subconscious all this time ready to be obnoxious.

She retrieved her car and went home. It was almost two by then, and she hadn't had any lunch. She coddled an egg and made cinnamon toast and pampered herself.

Pretty soon, she was going to have to face the fact that she would win Tad, and she would have to be a lady about it. And she was disgruntled that her mother had been such a stickler about manners and obligations.

She went upstairs and took a nap. And she dreamed that she had indeed won Tad, and they were in formal dress at the hotel for the final big dance. She didn't recognize the hotel and she wondered why she'd chosen to wear her high-school prom dress, which had been a putrid choice she'd insisted on over her mother's dead body. And her hair was wet and looked like seaweed.

J.R. was leaning against the wall in his jeans and hard hat and the women were fighting over him. Two of them had fallen to the floor and were struggling there. Jan was trying to see who they were, and Tad was trying to get her out to his car. That seemed so . . . juvenile.

And she wakened.

It was some great relief to know she'd been dreaming. If she thought the dream was juvenile, so was she! Why was she acting this way? Probably because she had a crush on J.R. She had never been in love, although she had on occasion been "in love" with some inappropriate male.

She remembered the summer after her junior year in high school, and her mad passion for a biker. And how amused Junior had been. He had said, "It's the motorcycle that appeals to you. It's the noise that grabs you. It sounds like the rider has power. Wait until Claude gets off that bike and you'll see a real disappointment."

Fortunately that had never happened. Claude was very like the old cowboys who wouldn't walk but always climbed on a horse to go any distance, long or short, like riding between the house and the barn. So Jan still occasionally had a poignant thought for Claude.

What was she going to do about Tad?

That depressed her so, and she felt all alone with no one to advise her or comfort her about this new disaster in her life. Actually she had never liked anyone interfering in her business. She had always kept her turmoils to herself and she *had* solved them all eventually. She would solve this, too, after she'd chewed on the problem for a time.

She thought she'd get a cat. Mrs. Witherspoon's cat tended to go home. He didn't mind sitting on strangers' laps since he'd been fixed and didn't rove,

The more
you love romance . . .
the more
you'll love this offer

FREE!

Mail this heart today! (see inside)

Join us on a Silhouette® Honeymoon
and we'll give you
4 free books
A free Victorian picture frame
And a free mystery gift

IT'S A
SILHOUETTE HONEYMOON—
A SWEETHEART OF A FREE OFFER!
HERE'S WHAT YOU GET:

1. Four New Silhouette Desire® Novels—FREE!

Take a Silhouette Honeymoon with your four exciting romances—yours
FREE from Silhouette Reader Service™. Each of these hot-off-the-press
novels brings you the passion and tenderness of today's greatest love
stories . . . your free passports to bright new worlds of love and foreign
adventure.

2. A Lovely Victorian Picture Frame— FREE!

This lovely Victorian pewter-finish miniature is perfect for displaying a treasured photograph. And it's
yours FREE as added thanks for giving our Reader
Service a try!

3. An Exciting Mystery Bonus—FREE!

With this offer, you'll also receive a special mystery bonus. It is useful
as well as practical.

4. Convenient Home Delivery!

Join the Silhouette Reader Service™ and enjoy the convenience of pre-
viewing 6 new books every month delivered right to your home. Each
book is yours for only $2.24* each—a saving of 26¢ off the cover price—
plus 69¢ postage and handling for the entire shipment! If you're not
completely satisfied, you may cancel at anytime, simply by sending us
a note or shipping statement marked "cancel" or by returning any
shipment to us at our cost. Great savings plus total convenience add up
to a sweetheart of a deal for you!

5. Free Insiders' Newsletter!

You'll get our monthly newsletter, packed with news about your favourite writers, upcoming books, even recipes from your favourite authors.

6. More Surprise Gifts!

Because our home subscribers are our most valued readers, when you
join the Silhouette Reader Service™, we'll be sending you additional free
gifts from time to time—as a token of our appreciation.

START YOUR SILHOUETTE HONEYMOON TODAY—JUST COM-
PLETE, DETACH AND MAIL YOUR FREE-OFFER CARD

*Terms and prices subject to change without notice. Canadian residents add applicable federal and
provincial taxes.

© 1991 HARLEQUIN ENTERPRISES LIMITED

Get your fabulous gifts ABSOLUTELY FREE!

MAIL THIS CARD TODAY.

DETACH AND MAIL TODAY!

PLACE HEART STICKER HERE

GIVE YOUR HEART TO SILHOUETTE

Yes! Please send me my four Silhouette Desire® novels FREE, along with my free Victorian picture frame and free mystery gift. I wish to receive all the benefits of the Silhouette Reader Service™ as explained on the opposite page.

NAME _____
(PLEASE PRINT)

ADDRESS _____ APT. ____

CITY _____ PROVINCE ____

POSTAL CODE _____

326 CIS ACEY
(C-SIL-D-01/91)

Offer limited to one per household and not valid to current Silhouette Desire®
subscribers. All orders subject to approval.

SILHOUETTE READER SERVICE™ "NO-RISK" GUARANTEE

—There's no obligation to buy—and the free gifts remain yours to keep.

—You receive books before they appear in stores.

—You may end your subscription anytime by sending us a note or shipping
statement marked "cancel" or by returning any shipment to us at our cost.

START YOUR
SILHOUETTE HONEYMOON TODAY.
JUST COMPLETE, DETACH AND MAIL YOUR
FREE-OFFER CARD.

If offer card below is missing write to:
Silhouette Reader Service,
P.O. Box 609, Fort Erie, Ontario L2A 5X3

**Business
Reply Mail**

No Postage Stamp
Necessary if Mailed
in Canada

Postage will be paid by

SILHOUETTE READER SERVICE™
P.O. Box 609
Fort Erie, Ontario
L2A 9Z9

DETACH AND MAIL TODAY!

but he did prefer the Witherspoons' house. She'd get a cat.

The phone's ring almost cracked Jan's headachey skull, so she picked it up with the first ring. It was Peggy.

"Yeah? What's the matter?" Jan asked.

Peggy said with interest, "Your highway Lothario called and said to meet him on his porch at eight-thirty. I tried to tell him that you weren't here, but he hung up. Who was it?"

"A . . . neighbor."

"Junior?" Peggy's voice had picked up.

"It's probably about the cat."

"What cat?"

She'd said the first thing right off the top of her sick head, and how was she to know what cat? "I'm getting a cat, maybe."

"From where?"

"I'm not sure. Will you excuse me, Peg, I've got a hell of a headache."

"Oh. Yeah. Well, I hope you find a good one. Cats are strange."

Jan agreed, and they hung up.

Her headache was better, if she didn't lean over. And she ate a very light supper, making exotic canapés and messing up a lot of food and most of her smaller dishes. She understood that she was killing time until J.R. came home from work. When she noted that, she also saw that she was setting aside samples of the canapés for J.R. Was she trying to tempt him?

No. She needed to chide him about his manner. He was really quite forward. He should watch his language, his choice of words. He was far too racy in the way he talked to ladies. To her.

When it was almost time to meet him on his back porch, she put on a long, soft blue dress that made her eyes really big and noticeable. She went barefoot and picked her tender-footed way over to his back porch.

Naturally as she sat on his back steps Mrs. Witherspoon's cat joined her, consenting to sit on her lap. But he licked and licked and licked, shedding hair all over her dress. She put him aside, but he would be on her lap. She even stood up for a while, hoping to discourage him, but he just waited.

In the deep dusk at 8:29, she finally sat down and accepted that the cat would be on her lap. But as she played with the black fur, she decided that she would pretend to be asleep. It had actually happened once and it had worked out quite nicely.

She thought of her few yoga lessons where she'd learned to relax. To be plausibly asleep, one had to be relaxed. She relaxed.

He drove into his driveway, and she was lying back on the steps, her head against the top step, one arm along the next stair, her bottom two steps down, and one bare foot now on the walk. The other leg was bent sideways to accommodate the damned cat. Her eyes were closed, her hair carefully in disarray.

He expected her to be there and saw her immediately, for he coasted quietly into the yard where he generally parked. He got out of the truck carefully and gently closed the door. She had a hard time not smiling. He was going to kiss her again. He was a shrewd and crafty man. Shame on him, she thought purely.

She could barely hear the whisper of his cautious steps across the grass as he came over to her and just stood there. She didn't dare peek to see why, then he carefully lifted the cat away. And he didn't do anything else. Why not? She almost peeked when she heard the odd rustling. What was he doing?

Then she heard his boots carefully scrape and she realized that he was taking off his work boots. More cautiously she listened, about to go crazy with her lax position and her pretend sleep. What was going on?

She heard his silenced breaths! And a thrill went through her stomach and the insides of her breasts and along her back and she twitched just a bit.

He went absolutely still.

She concentrated on breathing normally. What was normal? Her breaths seemed a little too fast. She sighed to slow down and moved her head a little, managing a tiny, quick, one-eyed peek at the sidewalk. Against the inside of her closed eyelid, she realized that he was standing there bare-legged.

Didn't he have on any clothes?

Very slowly he sat beside her, near her knee, on the step by her hip. And he leaned over her, his breaths shallow and quick, and he kissed her, hardly touching her lips. But with his lips still barely touching hers, his hot tongue touched that sensitive flesh with the lightest electrifying flick.

She about went crazy, but she held very still and did a brilliant job of being relaxed on the outside. Inside she was going berserk. It was amazing. She'd never, before that week, realized that she was a sensual woman. Why could J.R. do this to her insides?

Did he know his nose was puffing fiery breaths on her cheek that way? His breaths were so hot. That alone would waken a dead woman, but Janet Folger continued to peacefully sleep. Yeah.

He moved like a sneak and put his hand near her side right there beside her breast. She knew how close it was because his hand was as hot as his breath and radiated heat. He was going to grab her. She sighed again. And with her lips parted that way, he stole another kiss that got squishy and his tongue touched inside her lips.

Any woman has a limit, and Jan's tongue just went right out and touched his back. She then murmured as if in a dream.

In a husky voice he mentioned, "You're a fraud."

"J.R.?" She opened confused eyes.

"I drove around the block not two minutes ago, and looked through the Severs's yard, right through there, and you were sitting up. You couldn't have gotten that sound asleep in the time it took me to get two blocks."

She stared up at him, wondering what to say to that. He was grinning very smugly.

"If you wanted to be kissed, you didn't have to go through the charade."

"What a rude person you are."

"I know."

With Mrs. Witherspoon just next door, their exchange was very quiet. Keeping her eyes on his face, she asked, "Are you naked?"

"I can get that way very quick."

"I heard you taking off your clothes."

"They stink."

"You smell . . . used," she agreed.

"If you knew what all this body has had to do today, you'd understand it most certainly has been used." He smiled into her eyes, then he looked down her face and around that way as if he was memorizing her pores. He offered: "I understand the smell of men's sweat keeps women's periods regular. The *National Geographic* did a study. I'm available to be around you if you need any help in that way.''

"How kind.''

Their faces were only about three inches apart. His eyes were amused. "I remember when you first started your periods. You were so damned superior.''

"True,'' she admitted modestly.

"You acted as if you were Mother Earth.''

"It's a big step in a woman's life. My dad gave me my first real watch. He said it was an important time for a woman. Since he had admitted I was mature, I asked to drive the car. He said I was too young.'' She had reached up and was playing with his hair.

J.R. sighed. "Men never have any recognition.''

"Tough.''

"But we know how to cure headaches.''

"How did you know I have a headache?''

He frowned. "You do?''

"A killer.''

"Aww.'' His voice was sympathetic.

"I had to come home from the office. It must be the weather. It's sinus.''

"Where's it hurt?'' He put his big hand on her forehead.

"Here.'' She moved his hand to the top of her head.

"That's stress.''

"Stress?'' She frowned, unbelieving. "I haven't anything to be stressed about.''

His glance came back to her eyes. He was very close and his gaze was gentle. "You're stressed because you know you made a big mistake in betting five hundred bucks on Tad.''

"Bidding,'' she corrected.

"Yeah. Bidding. You're getting nervous because you know you'll have to put up with him for a whole weekend, and it makes you sick to think about it."

"You don't like Tad."

He was surprised. "Me?"

"Yes."

"No."

"Outside of the fact that it galls you that I be—bid five hundred on him, and only four dollars and fifty-one cents on you, what do you have against a gentleman like Tad?"

"There are gentlemen about whom I have no objections at all. Tad is a loser. He's at the top of his appeal. He'll go downhill from here on out. You ought to let Silthy have him. She is more tolerant than you."

"I'm a very *tolerant* woman! I don't know *why* you always have to find fault with me!"

"Well, I don't just harp on one fault, you have to admit that. I find your variety stimulating."

"I don't want a nit-picking man."

He turned generous. "You're really a pretty normal female."

"And I want a man who'll worship me."

"Think how hard it would be to get around the house, if some yahoo was always on his knees, worshiping you and getting in your way."

She laughed.

"Tell me you wish you'd put the five hundred on me."

She smiled back at him, then said, "You're so competitive."

"With the things that count."

"What things?"

"Jobs, cars and women."

"Listed right after cars. That's really exciting."

"I'm still young and juicy. I understand that after a guy's thirty, that rating begins to fall. The Super Bowl still comes first. Then there's cold beer, fishing, sandlot baseball, and things like that. And after forty, women come further down the list, but they probably still rank before mowing the lawn."

"The only reason we still put up with you, is that we haven't figured out a substitute."

"See? Even now you say 'substitute,' which means you can't give up the real thing. What's this argument doing for your headache? Distracted you enough?"

"It's gone."

"Now what 'substitute' could distract you like that? But if you'd still had it, I'd get you over to the clinic. I was worried you might have chilled last night. You went home before I could get you warm."

"I didn't chill. It was a warm rain."

"Speaking of the rain, you should have seen the site. We should have just stayed home. Some of the dummies got their vehicles stuck right off, and we had a hell of a time getting them unstuck." He moved his head once in a half shake over the idiocy of a few strays in his gender. "Well, Buttercup, have you eaten?"

"A little."

"That's probably another thing wrong with you, you're too skinny." But he was looking at her chest. "Just look at that toothpick arm." He picked it up and quite cleverly put that hand behind his head, and he kissed her again. "I always kiss women who put their hand behind my head."

"That seems a risky thing to do."

"I always do it on my back porch and not too many women show up here. You did see the sign that warns women of that happening?"

"Where?" She didn't look around, she just looked at all the lights in his eyes, which she couldn't possibly see because it was getting so dark.

"The sign's over there."

"Oh. I'll pay attention."

He kissed her before he again asked, "Have you eaten?"

"I have some canapés for you."

"Go get them. I have something for you."

"Oh?" She was cautious about asking what that might be.

"I'll surprise you." He stood up. He was wearing his undershorts.

Her insides quivered, but she knew she appeared quite calm, except that as he drew her up, her feet became confused, and he had to hold her while she reoriented herself. She did that without turning a hair, as if she'd planned to tangle her feet. She pushed at him enough to show that she didn't need any help. "I'll be right back."

"I'm looking forward to it."

She asked, "How do you know what kind I've made?"

"What . . ."

"Canapés."

"I'm looking forward to your return. Need any help?"

With the way that he was dressed, and even with the dead dark of night, she knew full well that he ought not be running around the neighborhood in his drawers. She glanced down him and mentioned that. Then the full impact of his masculinity was such that she lost her train of thought and simply enjoyed the view.

He smiled. "The canapés."

"Yes." And she trailed off toward her house.

She did wonder if she wouldn't be smarter to stay at home. He didn't need the silly frivolous bites of nothing she'd prepared. She could phone him and tell him her headache was back.

He'd probably take her screaming and kicking out to the twenty-four-hour clinic.

And she wasn't such a coward. She'd handled Junior all her life. he was no threat to her. When the microwave buzzed, she took the canapés out and carried the hot plateful over to J.R.'s back porch.

He hadn't changed; he was still in his underwear. Her steps slowed. He was sprawled just about where she'd left him. He had a cold beer in one hand and he was watching her approach. She felt a thrill of danger.

Danger?

She sat, with studied indifference, reasonably near to him without appearing to crowd him. She did that very well because he objected, "I don't smell that bad."

She grinned at him. "I was giving your elbows room. I've watched you eat."

"You said my mother would be proud of me."

"She is."

"How do you know that?"

"I see you." She draped his lap with a large, concealing dinner napkin. "But I think she might object to some of the innuendos you slide in."

He laughed. Then he surveyed her plate of delicate bits and asked suspiciously, "What are these?"

"You're supposed to say, 'Why, those look delicious.'"

"They look like table leavings." But as she reached to snatch away the plate, he dexterously blocked her hand by catching her wrist and holding it firmly. His other hand picked up a bit to taste it with great caution. Hesitating, almost putting it into his mouth, then taking it out to look at it again suspiciously.

Tad wouldn't have handled that the way J.R. was doing. J.R. was a hambone.

Chewing, he commented, "My God, Verbena, you've improved. The last hors d'oeuvres you fed me were flat rocks, mud and leaves. This is much better. I can chew it."

She looked patient.

He nodded. "They are delicious."

"That's all?"

He stopped to kiss his fingers. "Excellent."

"You don't like them."

He squinched up his face and asked, "Yummy in the tummy?"

And she laughed.

He fed her one or two, and she nibbled in a languishing invalid way. But then he opened up the insulated box and withdrew an already sliced pizza. She agreed to one small slice. He uncapped a beer and set it by her, then uncapped another, drank half with a big sigh and looked back at the tray as she was taking her second slice.

She ate her share and fought over the last bit of pepperoni, which they split. She even had another beer.

"See? Your headache was starvation. It wasn't stress, after all."

They lay back on the step edges and looked up, past the black leaves at the blue-black sky, and were contented. She stretched, feeling right. Then, behind a quick fist, she belched in a very unladylike way.

He reached for her and rolled her over on top of him, saying, "You need to be burped." And he patted her bottom and jostled her as she struggled and protested.

He burped. And that was cause for hilariously smothered laughter. She said, "You're very immature."

"I'll be nice and juicy all my life long—"

"—in a home for idiots." She finished it for him.

"But we'll have fun."

Did he mean with the other idiots or with her? "I'll probably live all my life right here in that house. I think I'll get a cat."

"A cat? Why would you want a cat?"

She examined her fingernail in the almost pitch-darkness and then raised her camel lashes so that she could look at his eyes. "I'm a little lonely," she said rather pitifully.

"Well, after I start my business, I'll be just next door, and we'll have time to talk over the back hedge and get acquainted."

"If we aren't acquainted already, what am I doing lying on top of your body?" She meant to be ironic, but with her consciousness drawn to his body with her words, the most amazing thrills shivered through her body in odd and hidden places. That concentrated her attention on her front, which was pressing so intimately against his hard chest.

"Steps are a hell of a place to make out."

She could feel the rumble of his voice in her chest. His hands moved up her sides and he was sneakily doing a very practiced feel-up of her here and there. She said, "Let go."

He spread out his arms to his sides and counted, "One, two and three. There. You had your chance." Then he wrapped his arms around her and curled his body as he parted his knees and her feet and legs eased down between his legs until her pelvis rested just above his in a very shockingly intimate manner.

She gasped, "You've done this before."

Kissing along under her chin toward her ear, he murmured, "Eaten on the back porch?"

"Fooled around on steps."

"Steps have never turned me on."

"With a woman."

"They weren't that old." He countered.

"Who?"

"Hmm?" His mouth took hers. It was exactly that way. He didn't just kiss her mouth, he took possession.

And she wondered who else was bidding on J.R.

"I always wanted to play doctor with you. Why did you let Peter see you? That's always nagged at me. Was it his name?"

"I've already told you why—he wasn't dangerous. He didn't scare my stomach the way you did."

"Scare your *stomach?*" He turned them so that he had access. "What do you mean 'scare your stomach?'" He put his big hand on her stomach.

"Well, you still do it."

"Do... what... to your stomach?" He encouraged as his hard hand rubbed a nice swirl on her.

"That's the only way I can describe it. You kiss me and my stomach gets odd. It's like the feeling when you swing too high. Or you think you're alone and you're going to do something rash, and you find someone watching you. It's very similar to being scared."

He grinned like a Cheshire cat and said, "Good."

"You like scaring me?"

"I'll show you why you feel that way."

"I think I ought to go home."

"Not yet." He was sure.

"Are you trying to seduce me?"

"Why would you feel I would try that?"

"Because of your hands, which are almost feeling me in a shocking manner of impropriety."

"Huh?"

She simplified it: "You're getting fresh."

"Does it scare your stomach?"

"You make me a little dizzy," she admitted.

"That's genetic," he whispered hoarsely in her sensitive ear, his hot breath sending goose bumps all over her, inside and out. "You've always been that way."

With difficulty, forming her lips carefully, she replied, "I won the spelling bee over you in the segregated days of boys against girls."

"So," he dismissed it. "You can spell."

He licked his lips by her ear, and the sound was so hungry that she shivered in a delicious way. "You could kiss me again."

"Thank you."

"You're welc—" His kiss was quite remarkable, and her brain cells swooned. Where had he learned to kiss that way? And she noted that his hand now covered her breast as it had been threatening to do. And it felt marvelous for that soft round to be kneaded that way. She heard herself make a strange, erotic sound in her throat.

He lifted his mouth from hers and pulled back an inch or two before he warned, "You're stoking my fires, do you realize that?"

Her wet lips smiled just a little.

"You're making me very hot, Rosebud, do you understand?"

She lifted a limp hand and gently mussed his mussed hair.

"It just so happens that I have protection for you. You did encourage me by pretending to be asleep."

"It wasn't the canapés?" She flirted with him. Waiting.

But he didn't know to follow that and ease into making love. He was earnest and concentrated. "If you don't intend to be had right now, you'd better untangle yourself from me and make your getaway."

She waited, but so did he, very tensely. As the silence stretched, she sighed in disgust. Then she pushed his arms off her and struggled to her feet. She stood there and looked down at J.R., who was a shambles, and again she said, "You're really very stupid." And she went home.

Seven

J.R. surged up from the steps, and wearing only his drawers, followed the wisp of pale blue cloth that was Jan. She went through the hedge, and he was buffeted by the swinging branches displaced by her passage.

Just the other side, in her yard, he grabbed her arm, turned her to him and kissed her as women dream of being kissed. He consumed her. He made her into a malleable mass of throbbing desire.

She gasped, "What about the woman you want? Your dream?"

He growled roughly, "You're my dream."

She melted to him.

Holding her in that manner, plastered up against his body with her toes dragging on the ground, he backed up carefully until he came to the end of the hedge and into the riotous disorder that had once been a vegetable garden.

There he stripped off her gown and laid it among the soft, thornless stalks of volunteer plants. He laid her down on that, followed her to lie beside her, and he kissed her again. He moved his hands to her breasts and found the secret medallion hidden between those soft mounds. In the night, he could only see that the treasure was plain and dark; not what it was, only that it was smooth.

With the secret talisman clutched in his hand and his fist pressed up between her breasts, he kissed her again.

Her brain swooned. How could just kissing be so euphoric? The meeting of mouths. How strange.

There was the sharp fragrance of crushed tomato plants, the tickle of long weeds and the earthy smell of compost. There were crickets somewhere, there were fireflies that floated, and there was silence. And he kissed her again in that same soul-shattering way.

In the odd sound of rush, a car drove by on the street in front of their houses. Someone on another street called to children. Children? She broke their kiss and twisted to look.

"What's the matter?"

Anxiously she asked, "Is anyone around?"

"No."

"You didn't look," she accused.

"I already did."

Yes, he would have.

In a roughened voice that was strangely gentle he commented, "You don't have on a bra."

She only then was really conscious of the fact that her bare breasts were in intimate contact with his hard, hairy chest. She opened her mouth and took a breath, but he already knew about her being half naked, so she didn't really need to comment or confirm that fact.

"You're so soft," he almost moaned the whispered words.

And there was the whine of a mosquito. "There's a mosquito," she mentioned distractedly.

"I'll keep you covered." He shifted, did that and kissed her again.

She became restless and wiggly. Her hands moved and her knees rubbed together as her back bowed, lifting her chest, straining closer to him. She began making little gasping noises, and he murmured, "This is just like my dreams."

"You dreamed hot dreams . . . about me?"

"Yeah."

"It wasn't dreams, it was telepathy."

That drove him crazy. His muscles were like rocks trying to hold her and not crush her. He groaned in agony and said, "I need you so bad."

There it was again. He was trying to make her ask for it. Didn't he know to just go ahead until she stopped him?

He leaned up on one tensed elbow and let his hand explore so gently along her body from her shoulder to her knee with pauses and swirls and kneading. He said, "Ah, Geranium, you are so beautiful." His finger touched her swollen lips. "So sweet. And look how red these dots are." He touched his finger to the small puffed nipples. "And here . . ." His hand slid over the silken lace of her panties as he cupped her mound then gently rubbed.

"Junior."

"Umm?"

"Go ahead."

His whole body gave a small jolt as if he'd touched a live wire. "Are you sure?"

She was silent. He waited, but his hand continued in its pettings and he leaned to kiss her again. And there was the soft accompaniment of the disturbed grasses as he shifted.

She helped with his embrace, her hands moving restlessly over his shoulders and head and along the sides of his face and back to his shoulders, pressing him to indicate she wanted him closer.

He was half on top of her and the only way to get closer was to put on the condom. He released himself from her clutching hands, and her little gasp of protest was an additional aphrodisiac to his libido, which was already on overload.

He skimmed out of his shorts and rolled on the condom. She was impressed that he could do that so skillfully in the pitch-darkness. That indicated . . .

He squatted down, ready. He took her panties off and tossed them aside. Then he lay down beside her and just hugged her to him. How did he know to do that?

When he'd stood up, she'd cooled a little with her nervousness and had to swat at a mosquito. Reality had intruded. What was she doing out there, lying stark naked in the weeds with Junior? But he lay beside her and just hugged her.

It was very quiet, and she was very self-conscious. Embarrassed. But she became aware of J.R. His breathing was so erratic. And he trembled. He was being careful of her. She could still, even *now*, she could still get up and leave. He was giving her that option.

She kissed him gently.

He shuddered.

She hugged him back.

And he let go the bonds of caution that had held him. The sexual sweat beaded his body, and he steamed. His hug changed, his kiss was soul-searing, and his hands moved in sensual scrubbings. He touched and searched her out. And the sounds he made were erotically inflaming.

He restrained himself, taking time to coax her to an unendurable pitch, then he eased onto her welcomingly eager body, and he sought her.

She was wild by then, and she helped him to break the barrier. As that was accomplished, she made a small sound and wrapped him in eager arms and legs, then curled her body and demanded release.

He'd planned a careful loving, but she got entirely out of hand. Their coupling became an exquisite romp of such scope that only his mouth smothered their gasps of intense pleasure and thrilling delight. They rode the wild wind of passionate ecstasy, and their free fall was interrupted by sensual pauses of aftershocks.

They lay sprawled in the crushed weeds amid the whining mosquitoes in the darkness of night, and they smiled.

It was some time before he could bring himself to gather the energy that words demanded, but he finally managed to whisper, "My God, Rosebud, you are something."

She whispered back, "I think you should have been a little more aggressive as we were growing up."

"For a woman who started playing doctor at age six, how did you survive until now?"

"I was waiting for you, you tomcat. How did you learn to put on a condom—and in the *dark*, that way?"

"I've been practicing for a week. I thought I might get you, and I wanted to be smooth."

"Have . . . you really?"

"Yeah."

"And you . . . never . . . ?"

"Not that I remember." Then he struggled up onto his elbows and he kissed her face very sweetly. "I needed you to know that Tad would be a loser."

"You expect me to do *this* with . . . Tad?"

"No, when he kisses you, and he'll try, you're to remember who you belong to."

"Uh—"

"Uh, who you love," he corrected quickly.

She monitored. "Whom."

"Me," he replied.

"No, it's whom you love."

"Yeah."

She swatted, saying, "I'm being eaten alive."

"I haven't really begun yet."

"By mosquitoes."

"That's what happens when a voracious woman drags a poor helpless man off into the bushes this way. How come you let the vegetable garden go to seed?"

She grunted, "You're really quite heavy."

"You took all my strength."

"But not your weight. Get off."

"You have a very short attention span. Not two minutes ago, you were wrapped around me, straining to get more of me, and you didn't complain about how heavy I was then."

She retorted snippily, "I got what I wanted, now run along."

"A masher. Does the Concerned Citizens Watch know about you? No wonder you dragged me back here into the bushes, Pussy willow."

"There you go, again."

"You called me a tomcat. The female version is a pussycat. It's your mind working overtime. You've always been a prissy piece. I remember some of the names you called me. I was shocked you knew them."

"Peter," she explained. "He collected things like that from his drunk Uncle Joe."

"I remember him," J.R. said. "We used to follow him from bar to bar and bet on which way he'd stagger."

"Now, that's like mocking a blind man. Times change attitudes."

"Yeah."

She confessed. "I never knew what Peter's words meant until I was grown. I didn't ask Mother after the first time, because she made me lick a bar of soap. Soap wasn't made to lick." She shared that knowledge.

"You must have been a trial to your parents. You sure gave me a hard enough time."

"I still don't know the meanings of some of the words. And there're jokes I'm only beginning to understand."

"What?" He nuzzled her ear.

"No."

"Yeah. I've heard that one lots of times."

"That wasn't a joke, I was declining to share those I don't understand."

" 'No' was never funny to me, either."

She asked, "Whom did you ask?"

"You."

"You never did ask me."

"All the time. I'd ask you to go to the cave with me, when I was so hot for you that I couldn't walk straight."

"I didn't know."

"Want to move over to my house?"

"Good grief!" Her whisper was almost spoken aloud. "J.R., what would Mrs. Witherspoon say?"

"She'd be excited. It would add spice to her life and maybe even *Mr.* Witherspoon's!"

"I must go inside."

"I am."

"I can see I'm going to be getting a great many innuendos now."

"Damn right."

"J.R., you are vulgar."

He kissed her very sweetly. When he lifted his mouth from hers, he asked, "Any complaints?"

She smiled, then laughed soundlessly. "I could box your ears, you've taken so long."

"I wanted you so hot that you couldn't stand not having me."

"But you've been next door for months."

"I knew exactly what you were doing the entire time. If any other man had been sniffing around, I'd have interfered. You've got to know I've been working myself to my knees. But I had my finger on the pulse. I knew what was going on."

"Why did you come back to Byford?"

"You have to know."

"But I could have been married any time along the way."

"Your mother kept me informed. If you'd gotten serious about any guy, I would have done something about it. You must know you've been mine since you were born. Mother brought me over and I saw you right out of the hospital. And I watched over you all along. You were trained by me to want only me. No other man would do for you."

"What conceit."

"No, I'm not conceited. I just trained you well." He moved just a little inside her, pressing, then he kissed her differently. He gave her sipping kisses, teasing kisses, touching her lips discreetly with the tip of his rubbing tongue.

She felt him thickening and her hips curled a little to accommodate him. She pretended not to be interested in being kissed, and his mouth coaxed. His hand moved to the side of her breast and his breath was heating.

Her whisper scoffed: "I can't possibly go through all that again."

He replied softly, "Of course not." And he shifted his body into a curve as his hand squeezed her breast up into a peak, then he bent his head almost impossibly as he stayed coupled and yet managed to suckle at her breast.

She stretched out under him, moving her shoulders, slanting her body to help his contortion. He pulled harder with his mouth, and she gasped with the sensation.

Then he separated from her very, very carefully. He discarded the used condom, turned on the hose a dribble to wash with the water still warm from the day's sun, then he rolled on another condom.

He came and lay down beside her and his hands were cool from the water. He heated very quickly. She allowed him to coax her into interest again. All the while, she mentioned that it was getting late, that the weeds were poking her, that the mosquitoes were annoying and that he was a greedy man.

He was not put off but agreed to everything with soft, hungry sounds. He pushed his face between her breasts and found the medallion. He took that into his mouth and sucked on it, trying to decide what it was. He released it, turned his face in that close nest, nudged the rounds apart and mouthed along, licking, until he reached a peak. Capturing it, he suckled vigorously. She had become silent and eventually she helped. But he lay back, stretched out and was still.

She waited expectantly, then she turned her head and looked at him, magnificently naked. He didn't do anything, so she raised up on one elbow and asked, "Are you all right?"

"Not yet."

"Why did you leave me?"

"I did all the work last time," he explained. "It's your turn."

She didn't reply. Then she looked at his body. She moved a hand over to cover him but that was inadequate. She used both hands, but even that didn't suffice. So she bent over and covered him with her hair. Then she nuzzled around him and she was smug that he gasped and whooshed and shivered. And she became quite bold and adventuresome.

She surveyed her new possession before she stroked and felt and investigated and tickled and licked and suckled and kissed, and he trembled and smothered moans and twitched and loved it. Then he helped her to mount him. He watched her serious face as she concentrated on doing that, and witnessed her blink of surprise and sassy grin when it was accomplished.

She experimented riding such a mount and reached around her bottom, pretending to search for him. She raised up a little and found the bottom of his stalk and she laughed.

He was rigid, amused, red-eyed and about wild. But he turned her gently, spreading the dress under her, and their ride was slower, more careful than the first time and their climax was shuddering.

"It really irritates me that you didn't introduce me to this form of exercise some time back."

"My mother threatened me." He carefully parted from her, and as carefully lay down beside her with his hand just under her breasts, his thumb between those mounds and touching the medallion.

He laughed gently. "You were worth all the agony of the wait. You are really a lover, Hollyhock."

"Do you call me flower names because that way, you don't say another woman's name at the wrong time?"

"You are all the beautiful things in this world, but I can't call you charcoaled steak, now, can I? Do you know what you smell, right now? Take a deep breath."

She inhaled. "Smashed tomato plants."

"Do you remember that tomatoes were once thought to be poison and were used only as decorations? They were called Love Apples."

"I remember that." She smiled as they lay in contented sentiment. "It's a good thing you brought me out here by the garage. It's so late that any footsteps on our porches would be heard and noted."

"I'll wait here until after you've gone in. You're sure I can't come inside with you and give you a shower?"

"Good heavens! You know better than that."

"I want to sleep with you," he coaxed.

"I—" She stopped.

"You what?"

"I would like to, too, but you know we can't do it." The fingers of one of her hands played in his hair while those of her other hand moved in his chest hair, feeling his nipples.

"Are you trying to excite me? Give it up. I'm shot."

"It is exhausting, isn't it? I have never been so tired. But it's a very nice tired. I like making love with you, J.R."

"I always wondered if you went all the way with Peter."

"Now you know that I didn't, with anyone."

"I'm glad. You're so sweet." He hugged her closely.

"Oh, oh, that's the way this whole thing started. I'd better go inside. Thank you for a lovely time."

"You're more than welcome, Goldenrod. There's always tomorrow."

"We're going to do this again tomorrow?"

"And every spare minute until after next week. I want you so sated that you won't even allow Tad to dance with you."

"For a five-hundred-dollar bid on him, I ought to be allowed to *dance* with him! All you do is stand still and hug."

"What's wrong with my hugging?"

She laughed very low in her throat.

"Don't laugh that way. You excite me."

"Oh, my word. It *is* time to go inside."

"Soon now."

"You're outrageous. Cut it out. Let go, I must go inside."

"Me, too."

She warned, "If you don't behave, I won't kiss you good-night."

He was instantly still.

She kissed him sweetly.

He whispered, "God, Nasturium, you are magic."

"So are you."

She rose, picked up her rumpled dress and pulled it on over her head before she trailed off slowly to her porch, where she slipped silently inside.

With his hands behind his head, J.R. lay like a naked Adam in Paradise, contented in the crushed weeds and volunteer tomato plants, companioned by mosquitoes, and he smiled at the night sky. Everything was working out just as he'd planned.

It was a night without dreams for Jan. She slept the sleep of a surfeited woman who had been well loved. No wonder contented women tended to be a little plump.

In the morning, Jan stared into the mirror at her lazy eyes and smiled. She moved as if in a dream. Her breakfast was ambrosia, and her clothing gossamer. Her car would be a boat drawn by ribbons held by a swan. If she smiled, the reflection from her eyes probably would glint like diamonds.

As she went out to the garage, she caught sight of something in the weeds and went over to see what it was. Her panties . . . and over there were his drawers! She'd told him not to run around the neighborhood in his underwear, and he hadn't! She put the betraying garments in her garage, wrapped together intimately.

She drove downtown, wandered into her office and smiled at everyone.

Peggy asked, "What's with you?"

Jan raised her eyebrows one one-hundredth of an inch and inquired, "With me?"

"Are you drunk?"

"Of course not." Jan blinked a time or two and surfaced enough to remember where she was, and she also remembered that Peggy was one of the bid-trio. "Peggy, we're old friends. We've been through a lot together. I want to change my bid on Tad to—"

"You already asked Carol. You can't change it. Carol said it was the rule. She told you that. You know not to ask me. Who do you want to switch the bid money to?"

Frowning, Jan corrected, "To whom do I want to switch the bid?"

"Yeah."

"Why can't I switch it? It's my money."

"All bids are final. Carol told you that. You know if we started switching them, people would just go wild, changing their minds endlessly and giving us all kinds of grief. You can't switch bids. Who do you want to change to?"

Jan was cool. "If you won't allow it, why should you ask?"

"Don't hit on Minna. She'll only give you the same answer. She knows you asked."

"Does everyone in town know?"

"Of course not." Peggy was impatient. "We don't talk."

"You don't need to. You chatter enough among the three of you."

"Boy, are you hostile!" Peggy held her own shoulders and shuddered. "Tad giving you trouble?"

"Now, you know better than that."

"Listen, Jan, for the family reunions during the festival . . . There are some of us who don't have families here, so we're starting our own clan. Would you want to join us?"

Jan looked at Peggy. "Why . . . that's a good idea. Thank you. I'd love to."

"You can bring Tad along, if you want to. Or if he bores you, bring Junior."

"His name is J.R. What should I bring? What's the family name listed on the location board at the park entrance?"

"We've racked our brains. Any suggestions? We don't want to use a generic name. We need something that means 'the Leftovers' or something like that."

"How about the Clan Gathered?"

"Not bad." Peggy raised her eyebrows and smiled. "Anyone named Gathered? We don't want to confuse anyone. What other names are up for grabs?"

"Nothing. Smith and Jones are official and rather heavily represented."

"How about Nom de Plume?" Jan suggested.

"If you'd answered your phone in the last two days, we could have had this brilliant input earlier."

"I was busy. How are the bids going? Will we be buying any trees at all?"

"You will be amazed," Peggy promised.

"Well, I know about my five hundred. Anything else?"

"You'll find out after the festival."

"I'm glad you three are so reliable, but I find it very irritating at times."

"Fortunately there are three of us." Peggy bravely put her hand on her chest. "We give support and comfort for all the hate calls and nasty looks."

"I've done neither." Jan gave Peggy a startled look.

"No. Yours is a cold and shriveling look. Carol is still wearing long underwear, since your parting freezing look."

"I did that?" Jan was unbelieving.

"Just the mention of your name and she shivers and wraps her arms around herself."

"Good grief. Carol isn't so fainthearted."

"Call her."

So Jan did. She said, "Carol, this is Jan."

Carol said, "No. Don't beg. We can't."

"No, no. I understand about the rules. Peggy said I had frozen you when I last saw you, and it wasn't intentional. Did I hurt your feelings?"

"I thought I'd devastated you."

"Well," admitted Jan candidly, "yes, you did."

"See? I feel like an ogre."

"No. Just a willful and stubborn female who had PMS."

Carol laughed and then asked, "You going to the family reunion with us?"

"It's going to be such fun that people will desert their families and come to our tables. Who all will we have?"

Carol began to name some of the people. But after a time, Jan had to say quietly with a fake smile, "My boss just came in, I have to hang up. Take off the woolen underwear."

Carol asked, "Huh?"

Then about ten-thirty that morning, it started to rain. At noon, the cohorts all met at Dorothy's Do Drop Inn. Most of them kept umbrellas in their desk drawers. So they arrived at the Inn breathless and shaking off droplets.

It made for a rather chattery lunch and everyone was a little excited about the auction that would be held in six days.

Jan faced the fact that she would have to do something about bidding higher on J.R. than she'd bid on Tad. So she would have to give the bid trio a check. The sooner the better. How was she going to do that?

She'd have to get a bank loan. They held still for her car loan. She wasn't sure how they'd view a second loan. But a bank had money and it seemed the logical place to go.

So just after two on Thursday afternoon, Jan asked her boss if she could run over to the bank for a minute. Jan was told to go ahead. And she ducked over to the bank, running through the rain, getting damp, her umbrella threatening to turn inside out.

She asked for the mortgage department. She didn't have to wait too long before she was ushered into Phyllis Allen's office to see if she could get a loan on her third of the house or on her car. It would have to be for five hundred dollars. She would cough up five dollars in cash. That would give her five hundred nine dollars and fifty one cents on J.R.

Phyllis Allen was patient and explained that they couldn't make a loan on one-third of a house. Jan already had a loan for her car. Unless it was a life-or-death proposition, Jan ought not borrow more money until she was solvent. Why did she need it?

Jan declined to enlighten Phyllis. So she didn't get the loan. Disgruntled because she knew Phyllis was right, Jan left the office.

The next thing Jan knew there were people around who gasped in shock and looked beyond Jan. Jan was annoyed and said patiently, "Let me through. I have to get back to work."

The person in front of Jan said, "There's a robbery in progress."

And Jan was impatient, repeating, "I have to get back to work."

And a rough, rather excited voice said tersely, "Be calm, and nobody gets hurt."

Jan turned around and stared in indignation, noting there were several masked men. She called to their spokesman, "I have to get back to work. I won't be in your way. Just let me past."

"Don't move."

She straightened up and put her purse behind her. That made her damp dress cling, and one masked guy drew in a sharp breath. The third man made a growling sound at the second, and then by the door there was a little scuffle that upset everybody. There was the sharp command to be calm.

And Junior came inside. He had his hands up, and he said with quick care, "I'm no threat. I'm construction. That's my woman over there. I'm only interested in her. My word on it. Okay?"

"Okay." The guy's voice was hesitant. "Go by her, keep everybody calm. This'll only take a minute."

J.R. came to Jan and asked, "You okay?"

"This is silly."

He smiled just a little. Then he said to the first man, "I'm going to put my hat on her head. Okay? That's all. I don't want her hurt."

"If you all behave, nobody'll get hurt. Get down flat on the floor."

They all did that. Jan didn't have a choice. J.R. saw to that.

No bullets were fired. The tellers were quick to obey. Money was scooped, and the robbers left. Several cars screeched away... and it was over.

J.R. said, "Never sass a nervous man with a gun."

"Where did you come from?"

"It's raining. Construction can't operate in rain. I went to your office to take you to your grandmother's funeral, but they said you were over here."

"My grandmother died four years ago."

"I know."

"You wanted to get me to play hooky!"

He grinned. "Yeah."

"What a good idea."

And sirens came screaming.

Eight

Minna Walters, the third member of the bid trio, arrived at the bank with her cameraman and microphone. She was vibrating with excitement, and when she spotted Jan and J.R. she was ecstatic. With witnesses, that was close to actual live coverage of a bank holdup.

But the police made Minna wait out on the sidewalk in the rain until she negotiated to step inside and just take pictures for a TV news flash. Minna's point was, if everyone knew about the robbery, they would notice things more. Like people fleeing. That took up time.

Jan kept saying, "I have to get back to work."

And the police said, "We need to debrief you."

They took the people who were calm and observant first, so that made Jan the last one interviewed. She was a little testy, by then, but J.R. was with her.

"What did you notice?" the detective asked patiently.

Jan was not patient. "They were masked."

"Halloween masks?" His tone was unbelieving.

"Scarves," she replied as to a backward child. "They'd pulled them up to cover their faces." She showed with her hands how that was done.

Minna took pictures from across the way.

"Did you notice anything about their clothing? Or the way they spoke? Did they call each other by name?"

"They were dressed in—" she gestured "—men's clothing. Nothing outstanding. Hats. But it was raining. They wore limp hats. The kind you can roll up and put in a pocket."

"Very good."

"They were polite, but they seemed a little impatient."

J.R. mentioned, "She wanted to leave."

"How did you come to be in the bank?" they asked J.R.

And he told about going by Jan's office to encourage her to play hooky. The detective nodded understandingly. "So you were standing together?"

"Yes," Jan said. "And they made us lie down on the floor."

"No. We weren't together. I came to the bank to find her and saw what was going on. And I asked to come inside to be with Jan. They let me give her my hard hat."

"That's interesting."

"They were very nervous," Jan said.

The detective eyed J.R. "They were very careful of you."

J.R. smiled a mean smile.

The detective nodded. "Smart. They defused you."

"No," said Jan. "J.R. had his hands up and told them exactly what he wanted, and they simply agreed. He was no threat."

J.R. just smiled very faintly and blinked his eyes once like a lazy lion. The two men exchanged a look. Then the detective asked J.R., "Tell me exactly."

J.R. described the kind of clothing and that it was new. And he described the cars outside, the year, kind and condition.

The detective asked, "How'd you notice that?"

"I saw what was going on. One of the cars had to be theirs. Those are gone."

The detective instantly questioned, "License numbers?"

"No. I needed to get inside. Anyway, I had to leave something for you guys."

The detective shook his head at J.R., signaled a cop who came, took the descriptions of the cars and left.

"I gave the car descriptions to the first cop."

"Good. Ever consider being a cop?"

"No." J.R. shook his head. "It's too scary."

The detective laughed. "So's bulling your way into a bank holdup."

"She was in here."

The detective looked at Jan then, who was frowning a little and listening, and then he smiled at J.R.

"It all seemed fake," Jan offered. "Who would believe anyone would be that dumb?"

"Always take people with guns seriously," the detective advised. "Anything you can add?"

"One was excited by Jan. She turned around and put her hands behind her back and—"

"I was hiding my purse. The bank can afford to lose money, but I can't."

"Yeah?" the detective looked down the damp dress of the seated Jan, as he listened to J.R.

"One sucked in his breath and the talker said something to him—harshly."

"So we have a lover."

"No, of course not." Jan countered crossly. "No one said or did anything out of line . . . other than rob the bank." She gestured as she mentioned that.

The detective said, "Robbing banks is frowned upon."

She gave him a patient look.

After they'd been questioned a little longer they were allowed to leave, but as they walked away the detective called J.R. back for a private word. "Watch out for her. He could come looking for her. She'll be on TV."

"I assume you will be keeping tabs on her, too?"

The detective said, "Yeah."

When the detectives finally finished with the people, Minna had her chance at them.

There was nothing they couldn't talk about. J.R. described the cars again. But he didn't mention that last little bit about the one robber being attracted to Jan.

Minna was delighted with their interview. Finally released, the two went over to Jan's office. There, her co-workers knew about the bank robbery because someone had gone to investigate all the sirens and excitement. He'd seen Jan and J.R. waiting for their questioning, so Jan's boss knew where she'd been. By the time she and J.R. had told the same things over again it was almost five, and her boss said to run along. It was okay.

It was really raining. J.R. smiled. He followed her home, and by unspoken consent, they went upstairs in her house and to her bedroom to get out of their wet clothing.

"It looks just the same," he said as he began to take off his jacket.

She gestured. "That rocking chair's new."

"It looks old. Where'd you find it?"

"Up at the Amish sales in Shipshewana."

He sat in the chair and rocked a little. "I like it."

"Well, thank God for that."

"Come here and let me rock you." He took her on his lap and cuddled her. "You stressed? That was a pretty different experience this afternoon."

"It seemed so fake."

"As I remember, you tend to go through crisis pretty well."

"I'm a stoic," she said impatiently. "Do you know what I found in the vegetable garden this morning?"

He smiled. "Flattened weeds?"

"Our *underwear!*"

"That was absentminded."

She accused: "You walked home in the *raw*."

"Well, you *told* me I ought not run around the neighborhood in my drawers. I was only obeying, as always."

She scoffed in disgust, "When have you ever done anything I asked you to do?"

"Endlessly. Do you want me to take a shower? I'm not too sweaty today. We didn't have but about six hours of work in before it rained too hard. I'm really pretty fresh. Smell me. If you choke, I could shower."

"What a gentleman." Her head was on his shoulder and she turned her face up to look at him, so of course, he kissed her. She said, "Ummmmmmmm."

"You like being kissed?"

"Umm."

"You said that longer when I was kissing you."

She smiled.

"You're driving my lap crazy."

"Good."

"Let's just get this damp dress off you . . ."

"Ah-hah."

"Now, why would you say that in that way? Your dress is damp from running around in the rain, and I don't want you to catch cold. Did you think I had an ulterior motive in removing your dress, Miss Folger?"

"What are we doing in my bedroom?"

"This is where your dry clothes are kept, right?" He worked at getting her dress off.

"Why . . . I've misunderstood your motives!" she exclaimed. "I do earnestly beg your pardon. How can I ever rectify such an insult?"

"You're sitting on it." He took her slip straps off her shoulders, sitting her up with her arms to her side, then he lifted her hips and worked the slip off down her legs, and sat her back on his lap.

"The rectification?"

Somberly he explained, "The means to apologize."

"Uh . . . wouldn't that only confirm the fact that you have ulterior motives?"

"Interior ones."

"Your clever tongue! I never get the better of you."

"You get the *best* of me." He vowed.

And she laughed.

He sat back. "Now, do me."

It wasn't impossible to get his shirt and T-shirt off him, but she had to get off his lap to undo his sturdy high-topped work shoes and his socks. But he got to watch her working at him. He found that stimulating. And he noted that the medallion was stuck between her wiggling breasts.

She earnestly stood him up and got his trousers off, and finally his drawers, and he became gloriously naked. She smiled up at him from her kneeling position. She said, "Wow."

"What do you intend to do with me? I have no dry clothing here."

She considered. "I'll put on a raincoat and run over to your house. Anything you'd especially like to wear?"

So of course he said in a gravelly voice, "You."

Cautiously she inquired, "Do you have any protection? I meant to get some today, but I was delayed."

"I bought some on my own into town. I figured that if I could get you to play hooky with me, we just might need some."

She grinned. "Smart. May I put one on you?"

"I'd never last."

"Well, I would like to try." She reached out and bobbed him. "You seem ready."

"Around you, I've never been anything else."

"I have a solution." She stood up, took his hand and led him to her neat bed. There, she folded the spread back tidily and then laid back the summer blanket and the top sheet. She gestured, "Interested?" And she looked sassy.

"I could be coaxed."

She licked her lips and moved her head while she elaborately ignored him. She took off her bra, then half turned away to slide her panties down her legs and kick them away. She raised her eyes and found that he was watching quite avidly. She said, "I put our underwear from the garden into my garage. Do you know what the neighbors would have thought if they'd found underwear from a man and a woman out there in the garden?"

"What?" He encouraged her reply.

"Well, it would have been obvious, wouldn't it?"

"You probably saved our reputations. It was just a good thing you went out that early and saw the damning evidence by all those trampled weeds."

She agreed. "We have to be careful or we'll cause a scandal."

"As I recall, Begonia, you always had a very clever tongue when it came to explaining the most shocking of our adventures. Remember Mr. Applegate's watermelon that we 'saved' from marauding pirates? You were a little young then, but it was quick."

She slowly shook her head. "They didn't believe there were actually pirates."

"You gave a great argument for it."

"I got better."

He asked seriously, "Do you love me?"

She was totally taken aback. She blushed painfully and looked everywhere at once. She gasped a dozen times, and she couldn't think of any reply.

He was jubilant. "You *do!*"

She shook her head in tiny tremors about seven dozen times and never said anything.

But J.R. laughed in jubilation and hugged her to his hard, hot body. He lifted her effortlessly into the bed and followed right in after her.

Then he didn't give her any time to talk or think but just went right ahead and stimulated her desires until she was extremely concentrated on him.

Her sighs and sounds, her little twitches and wiggles, her hands and mouth kept his own attention riveted, and he made love to her.

He wouldn't let her help him with the condom, even though his hands trembled and he'd have had a little trouble even without her interference. She was fascinated. "Let me."

"Cut it out, Jan."

"Well, you have such interesting parts. I want to be familiar with you."

"Oh, yes. Now. Now, you can get as familiar as you like! But don't take too long."

However, he didn't really give her any say at all. He just kissed her while his position and strength laid her flat. Then he pressed in as he wanted, and he had her.

But she had him. She squirmed and slid and grasped him. And she rubbed and moved. He did try to prolong their mating, but she had her sneaky way with him and drained all his resistance away.

As they lay depleted, he murmured pensively, "I miss the smell of the squashed tomato plants."

She groaned, "How long did you have to search before you could say 'squashed' tomato? That's typical of your humor."

"You made love to me. That's typical of your humor. You allow me to think I'm in charge."

"But you are." And she kissed him with sweet gentleness.

He dragged out of bed, pulled on his discarded clothes and went for his own change. He returned with four shelf dinners for the microwave. And they showered, dressed and watched the evening news as they ate.

They witnessed their interview. The filmed J.R. watched Jan. Although he glanced at Minna, he never did look at the camera. And while most of the men would understand him going into a bank that was being robbed, he would melt the hearts of all the women who saw them on T.V.

But J.R. saw that Jan looked more delectable than ever, and a squiggle of alarm was born inside him. No telling what that bank robber might do about Jan.

He went back to his own house and returned with a supply of clothing. He walked past a startled Jan and took his things upstairs to her room.

Not surprisingly Jan followed to ask, "What are you doing? If you move in here, why should I have been so alarmed about the underwear we abandoned out in the garden?"

He asked in real curiosity, "Why do you keep referring to that mess of weeds as a 'garden?'"

Distracted, she shrugged. "It was always 'the garden' as we grew up. It's only been a mess of weeds for two years."

"Why don't you just mow it over?"

"Are you changing the subject?" she inquired.

"Which one's that?"

She shook her head. "You can't move in here. It would be too shocking. Mother would know in another twenty minutes by mother-radar."

"I'm here as your protection."

"From what?"

"The bank robber who gasped when you turned around."

"Oh, pish and tosh."

Very seriously he told her, "Any man in that particular, horrendously tense circumstance who could be distracted by a woman could well come visiting."

She was somewhat flippant. "I still have the can phone. All it needs is a new string."

"Our interviews were all over the television stations today. It began on Minna's first news flash and was probably on the late show as well."

She scoffed. "You're seeing ghosts."

"I don't want one of them to be yours."

She sighed with great patience. "You've always been dramatic."

"I'm going to be your second skin until those guys are caught."

She grinned like a pixie. "Is *that* what you've been trying to do?"

"Trying to get your attention is like trying to squash mercury."

"We're back to squash." She was patient, but just a little irked. "You've always been that way. Dictatorial."

"I love you."

She turned and her smile was blinding. "Do you?"

"Good God, woman, haven't you known all along?" He put out his arms to show her his exasperation.

"You never mentioned it."

He rubbed his face tiredly and dropped down on that good rocking chair. "You're a very stubborn, difficult woman. It just shows how much I love you that I'll put up with you."

She crossed the room to sit on his lap. "Tell me again."

"If you want me to tell you right now, you have to know where we'll be in ten or fifteen minutes."

And he was right as usual.

But then the phone began to ring. Everyone had seen the news. And briefly the pair was notable enough that they made CNN. Her parents called from Colorado. They were cheerfully glad to see her looking so well, they said. They weren't the least alarmed. Of course, they didn't know J.R. had moved in with her. That would have really joggled them.

Jan took the phone off the hook.

Back in the rocking chair J.R. observed, "You've got weird parents. Do you understand that? Who else has parents who think it was an adventure for their daughter to be so lucky that she was in a bank when it was robbed? No one. Just yours. Why am I so surprised you're the way you are?"

She sat on his lap and his arms enclosed her. "Why did you go into the bank? Why did you insist? You didn't need to come in there. You *asked* to be allowed to be inside. Didn't you do that for an adventure?"

In a show of constraint, he sighed through his nose with an excessively long breath and said, "You can't be that dumb."

"Why else?" She smiled a little and waited with her eyebrows lifted encouragingly.

With excruciating reluctance, he admitted, "I wanted to be by you."

"To share the adventure," she confirmed.

"To try to save your damned neck!"

And soft as a whisper of the wind, she prodded, "Why?"

"Because." He was really irritated.

"Tell me."

He put his hand under her chin and ungently jerked her face up to his and looked at her. Then he grated through his teeth: "Without you, I'd die. There. Are you satisfied?"

"I love you, too." She wound her arms around him and hugged him to her.

"I don't want you ever to throw that in my face, do you hear me?"

"That you love me?"

"That I was ready to die for you."

Her chin quivered and her eyes filled, and she said, "Oh, Junior. Really? I just thought you were being your nosy self. You always had to see what was happening. Do you love me that much?"

"Yes. But I don't want to hear any more about it, okay?"

"But I know," she said.

He warned: "Don't give me a hard time about it. I mean that."

"You could mention it occasionally. It would warm my heart and make all your faults fade...at least a little."

"My...faults?"

"Hadn't you been aware you have some faults...really, quite a few?"

"What?" he asked indignantly.

"You're very impatient, for one thing."

"Anybody who's ever known you, has had to've suffered from that. It goes with the territory!"

"You're not very romantic."

"I've proved that I am, a couple of times, just to-day!"

"That wasn't romance. That was exquisitely performed sexual intercourse."

"That was love!" he snapped.

And she bubbled laughter, taking his head between her hands and kissing his nose and his eyes and his cheeks. He moved his head to expose his mouth, but she ignored that as she said, "I love you in spite of all your faults. I'll help you to overcome them."

"How are you going to do that?"

"I'll mention them and direct you in improvement."

"I'm leaving." He shifted to rise from the chair.

Still on his lap, she clung to the back of the rocker, preventing his feeble attempt to escape. She exclaimed, "You don't *want* to improve?"

"No."

"Well, maybe I can balance things a little and allow some of your faults sanctuary, in exchange for concessions that you would allow me."

"Like what?" he asked suspiciously.

"Tolerance?" she whispered gently and smiled at him.

"I'll think about it."

Thoughtfully, she added: "And patience. I have trouble being open with my feelings. That's why I need the reassurance of yours."

"Honey, you can be assured all your life that I love you. It's never changed."

"Then why did you leave me so alone for so long?"

"I knew what would happen if we were together as adults. We'd have been married five years ago, and we just weren't old enough. I'm here now, and we have all our lives ahead of us."

She demurred. "Not if you insist on going into banks that are being held up. I was appalled to see you storming the bastions. I almost fainted."

"But you knew why, didn't you?"

"No. Not until now. I thought you were just being your old inquisitive self."

He frowned at her. "Don't you understand that's why I always had to be with you? To protect you?"

"I know now. I'll be more careful."

He saw no point in that. "You attract trouble like flypaper."

"Now there's a romantic tribute."

He didn't reply to that; he just kissed her squishily and lovingly.

She murmured contented sounds and sighs. Then she asked, "Are your legs numb yet? Would you like me to move?"

"I like numb legs."

It was very strange to sleep with a man in her bed. He took up a lot of room. But in the cool, rainy night, she was warm. "I believe you beat having a cat."

"A cat?" He was incredulous. "Who'd want a cat?"

"Well, I don't believe I really do, I was just lonesome. But no cat could warm my back the way you do."

"I'm about to die of the heat."

"I warm you?"

"Who needs all these covers?" He flapped them up and down.

"Listen, buster, for what you're paying you can't complain."

He retorted. "Do you know what condoms cost? At the rate you're using them, I'll be broke before the year's out."

She sighed. "I suppose after that I'll be pregnant every year."

"No." He had his fingers between her breasts, feeling that medallion and wondering why he hadn't looked at it earlier that afternoon. He'd been distracted. "We can't do that until after we're married next week."

"*Next week?* We're getting married next *week*? I can't. I have a date with Tad for that weekend."

"You'll have to break it."

Quite logically she inquired, "How can I break a date with Tad when I paid five hundred dollars for it?"

"Now, that's ridiculous," he groused. "How are you ever going to explain all that to our kids?"

"I'd leave the explaining up to you."

He pulled back to frown at her. "You want me to tell our babies that you paid five hundred dollars of their great-grandmother's money to bid on another man, and only four dollars and fifty-one cents on their daddy? How do you think that will make you look in our innocent children's eyes? They'll think you're a flighty woman."

"That's possible."

"I dread having to convince those babies that their momma is a good and loyal woman."

"You're going to rub my nose in this all the rest of our lives."

He echoed her own recent comment with a theatrical sigh. "That is possible."

"You're a beast." She wiggled her fanny into his lap as she settled down to sleep.

"But a man does as he must."

She laughed, low and intimately.

"What are you thinking, you Jezebel, to laugh in that particular way?"

"How much I like having you in my bed."

"What a shocking thing to say, Miss Folger, when all I've heard is that your mother will throw a conniption fit the minute she learns of this scandalous behavior in her baby daughter."

"While the cat's away, the mouse will play."

His voice very husky, he asked, "So you want to play, do you?"

"I've played enough for today."

"You don't have to do anything. I'll just toy with you."

"I thought we'd overused the condom supply."

"I have some left." He assured her. "I bought extra . . . was it just this afternoon?"

She turned so that she could look at him over her shoulder. "I've been meaning to inquire as to just what you had in mind for this afternoon, when you lied to my boss about my grandmother dying and you having to fetch me out of there. What did you have planned that you had to buy an additional supply of condoms?"

"You'll have to wait for the next heavy rain to find out."

She laughed. She lay there in her virginal bed next to the heat of her childhood chum, and she laughed the deliciously taunting way of a woman with a man.

"When you laugh that way, you drive me crazy."

"You don't like it?"

"Darn you, you know what you do to me."

"What?" She encouraged his reply.

"Give me your hand."

But she moved her bottom against him instead. When he groaned, she turned over and allowed her own hand's independent verification. She said, "I'm a failure."

"Hardly."

"I've worked all this afternoon, trying to help you, and I've failed."

"Third time's charm." He coaxed. "Don't give up. Try and try again is an old-time motto that is priceless."

"I'd never realized that was about sex."

"What else?"

"Having known you intimately for about twenty-four hours, I'm surprised I hadn't realized it."

"Since you're responsible for my condition, it's—"

She corrected him. "I was lying here, trying to go to sleep—"

"—right that you take care of me."

"Well. I suppose if I ever want to get to sleep, I might as well give up and get busy."

"That's a good attitude," he commented. "Where do you plan to start?"

"Let me roll on the condom."

"No."

"If I ruin it, I'll buy the next box."

"Oh? You plan to do this regularly?"

"I'll see."

And she made him laugh.

Nine

On Friday morning J.R. was up and gone before Jan even really remembered that he'd stayed with her. He'd kissed her sleepy mouth and said, "It's still raining. I'll probably come back into town."

She'd smiled lazily. "Another of my already dearly departed is going to again bite the dust so that I can play hooky with you?"

"Naw. I can't pull that trick again for a while. I'll probably help with building the stage for the auction." He kissed her deliciously and growled, "You sure look tempting."

She whispered, "Help, help."

"Cut that out. You know a challenge excites me. I won't see you until noon. Going to Dorothy's?"

"Yes."

"I'll see you there." He said that over his shoulder as he left.

And she frowned. No one knew she was attracted to Junior. She'd never said a word. Well, she was a neighbor, and they wouldn't suspect he'd moved in on her. It would be like the announcement night. No problem. He'd just happen to be at the same place for lunch, and she'd be neighborly enough to sit with him. It would be all right. She wouldn't have to deal with any snickers or lewd remarks.

She moved her body in the bed and felt sated and luxurious. She smiled. What a greedy man. She wished he was back in bed with her. But he wouldn't be idle today and lure her into playing hooky. Darn. He was going to help build the platform for the auction.

That only proved next Wednesday would come, the auction would take place and she'd win Tad. That depressed her. Five hundred dollars would be wasted. Well, five hundred would buy a lot of trees. She just hoped her grandmother knew what all was going on with her legacy and could be entertained by all the frustrations and drama.

Then Jan remembered that her grandmother had always inquired about Junior. She'd smile about him and Jan's scoffing reports. She'd probably known all along that Jan was partial to J.R. Jan thought what a nuisance it was that *she* hadn't realized her attraction for her neighbor. If she had known, what would she have done? Probably botched the entire thing.

He'd said... he had said that he had been ready to die for her. She stilled and sobered. My God, she thought, how did a woman handle that kind of commitment? Would she be ready to die for him? She squinted at the ceiling and considered that, and she knew that dying would never occur to her. She would fling herself into whatever danger there was and depend on J.R. to save her. And of course, in order to do that, he would have to save himself first.

And he could. He could do anything.

She stretched leisurely, thinking of the things he'd done to her just recently. And her eyes glazed and her mouth softened and she nuzzled his pillow.

What a man. She remembered his concern about her chilling, about her headache, about her being in the bank during the robbery. And while he admitted to loving her enough to risk his neck, he pretended to himself that he had only a sexual hunger for her? Silly, silly man.

At noon, Jan was a little nervous seeing him at Dorothy's Do Drop Inn. Jan was very casual and indifferent when she saw him open the door and look around the noisy place. She hesitated in the middle of a comment she'd begun, in order to watch until his searching gaze found her.

And he made a straight line to her, never taking his stare from her. She tilted her head back to keep him in sight, and he bent down and kissed her. He hadn't even bothered to remove his hard hat. She sighed, but she did smile up at him.

Then she noticed the dead silence in Dorothy's, and that all attention was directed to J.R. He acknowledged them all: "Ladies." He found a chair and crowded in by Jan.

Well, he'd never been subtle. When Tim had grabbed her notebook out from under her books once in the fifty grade and spilled all her papers on the windy school yard, Tad had helped her pick up her papers, but Junior had run Tim down and sat on his chest making him yell an apology to Jan.

Now, J.R. sat squeezed in by Jan, taking up more than his share of the table, replying to the stupid tries for his attention from the women around him. Even the women at other tables were calling to him. And he was courteous. But he would turn his head aside and look at Jan over his shoulder in an excessively possessive way. His eyelashes were almost screening his hazel eyes so smugly that he embarrassed her.

In an intimate whisper he told her, "I hear your Great-aunt Susie is feeling poorly."

Snippily she retorted: "That's not surprising since she's been buried for something like forty years."

"You coming over to inspect the platform?" He growled the words. "You ought to." He paused before he said, "What happens in that room on Wednesday could change the course of your life."

"After I win Tad, I will be polite but distant with him," she declared. Then she glanced up into his hazel eyes and became a little faint.

He looked at his watch, lifting his arm that had to nudge her breast, he was so crowded. "I've got to get back. It's been a pleasure." He looked at her salaciously. "See you after work." He got up and nodded to the women whose gazes were glued to him. "Ladies," he said again. And he left. But at the door he turned back and, sure enough, he'd caught Jan watching him leave. He winked and was gone.

Somebody said in an excited giggle, "Why would Junior come have lunch with you?"

Very coolly, with only a faint blush that suffused her entire body, Jan replied, "He was reporting on the progress being made on the platform . . . for the auction," she added kindly. "The rain prevented him working at the site, so he volunteered to work on the platform for the festival.''

Everyone there had some duties concerning the event. She hadn't needed to elaborate.

"He could work on me," some idiot female voice said with a sigh.

"I'd show him how to spend a rainy afternoon," another offered. Then she explained naughtily, "Home movies."

And everyone laughed. Well, Jan didn't.

The rain continued.

The afternoon went so slowly that it was maddening. Jan finished everything she could think to do and finally attacked the files. At last it was five o'clock, and she could go over to the hall and see how the platform was going.

The hall would be used by several organizations during the weekend-long Mid-Summer Festival. The Garden Club would be first with its auction and dinner dance on Wednesday. But after that there would be exhibits by the Scouts and by a boating company. The fine arts groups would have a ballet, and there would be artists' exhibits hung for viewing. The platform being built would be well-used before it was taken down and stored until the next time.

Jan saw that Minna was there for her TV station, getting film on the volunteers at work. That scandalous J.R. had his shirt off, but he was still wearing his hard hat. Minna sneaked her cameraman around. J.R. didn't even notice. He was lifting a crossboard up, and the effort bulged his shoulders and pulled in his stomach so that the top of his trousers gaped very salaciously down below his hairy belly button. Any woman seeing that would want to rub her hand over his textured stomach and down into the loose top of his pants to find out about that lump lower down. Jan held her forehead.

Minna said, "Jan."

Jan lowered her hand and looked up. She asked, "Yes?"

And Minna just smiled.

The pair didn't get to Jan's until almost six. J.R. followed Jan home but he parked, as he always had, in his own backyard. He came through the hedge, over to her house, with some shelf-stored microwave suppers. He gave her a mind-spinning kiss and said, "Let's get the news. I want to know if they've found the robbers yet."

The police spokesperson said gloomily that they were following tips, and they hadn't yet made any arrests. That was ambiguous enough.

But the next film showed Minna's pictures of the auction platform being built and a marvelous picture of the half naked hard-hatted J.R. And watching, the picture's subject said disgustedly, "Aaarrrkkk!"

Jan said musingly, "I want a frame of that for a wall poster."

"Don't be dumb. You got me."

"You don't like groupies?" She looked at him in surprise.

"Not while I'm trying to deal with the woman I'm working to satisfy."

But then on the TV was a picture of Jan that was ethereal. She looked up at the camera, wide-eyed and curious, and any man would want to be the one she was watching.

J.R. sat forward and said, "She got you just exactly. I want that."

Jan said, "Good gravy, J.R. I have enough trouble with you, as it is!"

And he looked over at her the way he had at lunch. It was so *personal* for him to eye her like that. It was as if—

He stood, lifted her up out of her chair and carried her upstairs to her bed. So it was some time before she was able to eat supper. But he'd just proven that she'd been right about how that look . . . looked.

They went to bed early, but in the middle of the rainy night, she wakened to find him seducing her. She laughed in her throat and lay lax, allowing that. He loved the feel of her and took some time experiencing the different textures of her body and the different ways that he could enjoy those differences, with his hands and body and mouth.

She was too sated to have her passion captured, but she was welcoming to his. Her pleasure was in his.

On Saturday, it was still raining. J.R. got up as usual, but a phone call told him to forget going to the site, it was a quagmire. So he got back into bed. Jan questioned his right to do that, and he showed her the reason. She was astonished, amazed and astounded. So he had to explain the whole process all over again. He said she was a slow learner, and she laughed.

At seven they got up, showered, dressed and had breakfast. Jan put in some wash, and he added his. She had to wash the load a second time, his clothes were that dirty. They made up a grocery list and she went to shop, while he went to check his house before he went back to help with the platform.

Jan came home, put away the groceries, moved the washed clothes to the dryer, put in another load to wash and tidied the kitchen. She dressed and drove downtown to the hall to see what was needed for the auction. Some publicity pictures had been taken to snare people into coming to the Garden Club's Wednesday night dinner dance for the announcement of the winners in the silent auction. The tickets had been selling rather slowly.

But when Jan arrived at the hall, she found that the three phones had been ringing for a couple of hours, that the surge of interest was rather boggling the committee, and Jan was snared in to help take reservations.

By noon, it was obvious that they were going to have to get in more tables. By three in the afternoon, they were beginning to worry about fitting in enough tables. They were ragged and tired and jubilant. All this was for the Garden Club's tree project for the Mid-Summer Festival.

It was with some inner hesitancy that Jan helped nail up five huge poster pictures of the men who'd consented to be auctioned. And there was the one of J.R. with his blue shirt, hard hat and wink. Jan thought all the other men looked like Caspar Milquetoasts.

One of the granddaughters of a charter member of the Garden Club stood back to look at J.R.'s picture and smiled. She said in a moony way, "He makes me want to be hugged up—really close."

Jan looked down the girl's very female body and frowned. Then she confronted Minna, "See? You need to change my bid. Do you want J.R. to have to cope with something like that? It would terrify him."

Minna exclaimed, "So it was to be changed to Junior! We suspected that." But she just shrugged as she then said, "If the bid is high enough, who cares?"

Jan did.

Some flippant reporter wanted a picture of a dog sniffing the symbolic cardboard tree that would stand at the entrance on Wednesday night, but Jan was particularly opposed. "The trees are for clean air. We aren't doing this for dogs, we're doing it for people."

She was so earnest that she converted the reporter to the seriousness of the problem. On Sunday they found the reporter had composed an excellent article, having obviously done additional research, and there was a picture of Jan gesturing as she explained how badly the world needs trees.

With the bank robbery and the publicity of the Garden Club, Minna said Jan ought to run for mayor. Jan gave Minna a disgruntled look. But she asked for a frame from the tape of J.R., half naked and lifting that board.

Minna smiled and said, "We're printing copies to sell for five bucks each. The club will make a fortune."

After church on Sunday, the club met and tried to figure out how they were going to coordinate the doubled attendance to the auction. They were having to put people on a waiting list for cancellations. Jan watched Tabby dealing with all that, organizing it and parceling out duties to the club. And during a break she told Tabby, "You're brilliant at organization."

Tabby said, "Thanks. Jan, you see to the table flowers. We don't have enough to go around. Figure out a reduced centerpiece that won't look skimpy."

That proved one should never call attention to oneself under any circumstances.

But the worse thing for Jan was that there were additional bids on the five men being auctioned. She wondered who would get J.R. Probably that female who'd wanted J.R. to hug her "up close."

Sunday night long after the supper hour, as they wolfed down fast-food hamburgers, and with the "hugger" still in her mind, Jan asked J.R., "Are you susceptible to strange women?"

"What sort of strange women?" he asked cautiously.

"Unknown to you."

"Oh, I thought you meant like you. Have I ever mentioned that you're really—" He glanced over to see her eyes widening and her lower lip getting stubborn, so he sorted through words until he found: "—different? I've never met any other woman quite like you. Most women are soft and easy. You're...a...challenge."

"So you don't care for m—?"

"I like challenges. It's just that women are a whole 'nother race. I've been doing some extra reading on females and their workings, and if you have any questions don't hesitate to ask."

"Why did you do that?"

"I need to understand you," he explained. "You've always puzzled me."

"I'm perfectly normal!"

"Oddly enough...uh...*surprisingly* enough, you *are* within the 'normal' range. I would like to start a support group with the guys whose women are in that category."

"Support group?"

"Yeah. I probably know more about this kind of female than they do. The quirks and responses, that sort of thing." He was a little arrogant.

"So you've read up on me."

"I really prefer the hands-on investigation. I get more out of that."

She lowered her gaze to one side and tilted her head a little before she looked back up at him. "Hands-on?"

He shared knowledge. "It's like pottery makers. You throw the virgin clay on the wheel and form it. I could be a big help in a baffled-male support group."

"What would you tell them?"

"I'd look at the poor, puzzled bastards and say, 'Give up. Roll with the punches. Don't try to understand. Just go with the flow.'"

"That's what you think you do with me?"

He looked indignant. "Of course not, but most men who encounter women like you expect rationality. I don't. I just tell you what to do, know you won't do that, and then try to keep you from getting us both into trouble. That's why I put on the condoms by myself."

"And you think I'm weird?"

"Mind-bending," he agreed cheerfully. "I will never figure you out. But occasionally I see that glimmer of common sense in you that, if I could just capture it, we might build on it and make you rational. It's an elusive hope."

"You're a male chauvinist!"

"Well, with men trying so hard to get along with women, trying to be sensitive and tender and open, somebody's got to keep the flame alive."

"My God."

"Yep. Get upstairs, woman, you're in training."

"For what?"

"For me."

But he didn't have any complaints. She would stop here and there along the exercise and inquire if he was satisfied and he'd gasp, "Not yet!"

But when she then asked, "What am I doing wrong?"

He'd say in a euphoric groan, "Nothing!"

And when he was lax and gasping, sweat-slippery and trying to regulate his heart and lungs, she asked, "Are you satisfied?"

He just smiled and purred.

"So I'm no longer 'in training' and I am satisfactory?"

He mumbled, "So far."

"So far? What do you mean, so far?"

"Nuances. Graduate work."

"Well, let's get busy."

But he was out cold, or he appeared to be.

It was still raining on Monday. And Tuesday brought the inevitable jokes about building an ark, gathering the animals, and men who told women, "I have a ticket for the last place in the ark. If you want it, you have to convince me that you're willing to do your share to help replenish the earth's people." Well, women have good senses of humor and they're tolerant.

Jan left J.R. in her bed, sleeping flat out and never stirring. On work breaks, she garnered suggestions on what on earth she could do about spreading the table bouquets to grace double the tables. The suggestions cost money.

So she took home Chinese and sat with J.R. watching the news, which consisted mostly of flooded houses and boats on streets downtown or north of Byford. Then J.R. took Jan around her house as he opened and closed stuck doors and drawers that he'd planed or glued and fixed. He showed her a rattly doorknob that was now tight and responsive. And he had her note the faucets that no longer dripped. She was impressed and exclaimed very satisfactorily.

She asked J.R., "How am I supposed to stretch the table bouquets? We are blatantly chintzy with our budget. We'd rather have trees along the highways than flowers on all the tables."

"Our hedge."

She frowned at him, thinking he'd slipped a cog, then light began to dawn and she smiled. "You're brilliant."

He looked patiently modest.

Their hedge was huckleberry, which florists use as filler. The bouquets would just have more filler.

So the next day was clear, sparkling and Wednesday. The day of the auction. That morning, as people moved around in the early hours, getting the tables positioned, laying the cloths out and setting the places, Jan was there with the flowers.

In a side serving hall with two archways into the great hall, Jan worked at a table filled with a million empty fluted vases. J.R. had the day off for this particular project, to help her. It was too wet at the site, anyway, but he made a big deal out of being there for her. She loved it.

J.R. was soon lured away to help with running cables and testing mikes and doing other things. But he'd carried in the bundles of clippings he'd lopped off their hedge. And he came back to see how she was getting along. "You ought to sit down."

"Yes," she replied distractedly.

Or she said, "Shh, I'm counting."

Or she said, "Hmm?"

So he patted her fanny if no one was around, or he kissed the back of her neck, or he just said, "Need anything?"

"Eight hands."

"Why, I have those!" he exclaimed. "You told me that just last night!" And he'd stuff hedge clippings into vases until someone else would yell for him. He could fix anything.

It was while she was alone that she heard someone inquire, "Jan?"

She didn't even turn but said "Umm," and went on working.

"Remember me?"

For some reason she felt an odd sense of something about to happen. Her hearing went strange and she felt her head's turning took forever. She saw a man standing there, and she stared.

He wasn't much taller than she, but he was very masculine. His eyebrows were unusually thick and dark and his eyelashes were a thicket. She noticed that. His hair was neat and dark. He was tanned or Latin, she wasn't sure. And he was dressed in shirt and jeans and running shoes just like everyone else. She shook her head.

"I was at the bank." His voice was soft, and he smiled a little. "Remember?"

"Were you down on the floor, too?"

"No."

She thought: good grief, it was one of the robbers? How could he be so foolish as to be there? There were a hundred people in that place—but there wasn't anyone else in the hall.

She had the scissors.

He said in soft coaxing, "Let's go for a soda. I'd like to just talk for a while." And he smiled, seeming harmless.

"I have all these vases to fill. I can't leave." Where was J.R.—and then she knew that she didn't want J.R. in any danger. She couldn't risk him. She would handle this by herself.

She tried to see if the man was armed, as he had been at the bank. But if he did carry a weapon, it must be in his sock or in the belt at the back of his trousers. He didn't appear dangerous.

She said, "Sorry." And went back to work, very conscious of him standing there, so she knew when he moved.

He took her arm. "You've been working very hard. I've watched you here, this last week, and you could use a break. Let's go. My car is just around the corner. I want to talk to you."

"Look at all these vases. Talk to me here. Help me with this."

"Someone would come."

Yeah. J.R. And what would happen? She turned to face him. "My mother said I was never to get into a car with a strange man. You have to know about that. You were raised to have manners. Do you have any sisters?"

"No."

"Well, your mother would have—"

"I was a foster child," he replied. "I had many homes."

"Did you. Do you think that's better than an orphanage?"

"Who knows? Come."

"I really need to stay here," she said earnestly. "I have work to do. I don't know you. I don't want to leave here."

"If we stay here, the hard hat will come back."

"He's my neighbor." She minimized J.R.'s closeness to her.

"He stays in your house. There is only one light upstairs."

"You've been snooping. Mrs. Witherspoon doesn't even know."

His voice was gentle. "I don't want to harm him. Let's go. I just want to talk with you, to become acquainted."

"That isn't a good idea. As you have found out, I love that man. I don't want to become acquainted with anyone else. You need to find a woman who is free to be friends with you. I am not. Go along now. I'm very busy. This must be done."

"Please."

"Are you trying to irritate me?" She frowned at him. "I am being very civil to you, but you're annoying me." She indicated the empty vases. "All of these have to be done in time. I'm responsible!"

"I have this planned. Come."

"No." She turned fully to face him and clutched the scissors behind her back.

He looked at her and smiled. "You look as you did then at the bank. You're very pretty."

She caught a glimpse of someone who almost came through the door, but backed...or was pulled quickly away, out of sight. Were they aware of her problem? Or had they simply been distracted? Had it been J.R.? She couldn't allow J.R. to walk in on this. He would attack. He might be hurt. She could handle this gentle person. He was no threat. She really had to get him out of that place and on his way.

"All right, I'll go out the door with you," she said in a rather loud, exasperated way, in case it was one of the Garden Clubbers there who was aware of this confrontation.

He smiled sweetly. But as she started toward him, he said, "No. The back way."

She stopped. The scissors were behind her. If she turned, she would have to shift that hand so that the scissors were concealed. She stared at him. "I don't want to go out the back way. It's scary."

"I'll be there. Nothing will happen to you. I just want to talk."

"I have nothing to say." She listened. People were moving around beyond the wall. There was talking. There was steady hammering. How could all those people be over there, and no one know this man was accosting her, trying to get her out of there through the back way?

She prayed for anyone but J.R. Anyone else coming through the door and Jan could say, "I have to get more flowers," and she could run, but J.R. would recognize that this man was not supposed to be here. And he would look at Jan and see that she was unnerved and he'd go for the guy.

"Let's go," he said softly.

"I guess you'll have to shoot me, right here."

"I don't want to shoot you, Jan. I want to talk to you."

"Who can trust a bank robber?"

"So you do know it's me."

"You told me you weren't on the floor. The only ones standing were the crooks."

"We needed money."

"There are other ways of getting it."

Beyond the robber's back, a hand came around the edge of the opening and waved down once and disappeared. Now what did that mean? Get on the floor? Or go on out the back?

She turned and put the scissors in front of her. She walked bravely ahead of the bank robber. Someone was aware of her plight. Who? Not J.R. He wasn't this subtle. She got to the next opening and as she came level with it, J.R. reached out and *snatched* her through the opening and down on the floor.

All hell broke loose. The bank robber was face-down on the floor being handcuffed by a great big man who was red-faced and snarling. And women were high-voiced and questioning. And men were shouting and people were running around and it all was really fascinating.

One excited male was saying, "—and we went right on trying to hammer naturally."

So they had known she was in trouble.

Under her, with his arms squeezed around her, J.R. said, "My God," at least fifty times. His eyes were red with tears and his grip on her was a little painful.

"I didn't want you involved," she told him very earnestly.

"I had to be. Under the circumstances, if anyone else had reached for you, you'd have panicked and the bastard would have, too. I had to get you out of there."

And they each knew Jan had risked her life to protect J.R., just as he had done for her at the bank. It was an emotional realization.

Jan's voice was breathy and a little high. "Was it you who almost came into the hall?"

"Yes."

"I'd hoped not."

That made him indignant. "Why wouldn't you want me to save you? I'm your man."

"I didn't want you hurt."

"God, but you're stupid."

"I love you, too."

"At least you recognize the symptoms." He grated the words. "It's just the way I've told you—you attract trouble like flypaper. How will I survive?"

"I told him he'd have to shoot me there. I couldn't go with him."

"We heard everything," J.R. told her. "The table was wired. We've had you under close surveillance since the bank robbery. That was one reason I moved in with you."

"The *table* was bugged?" she gasped. "Good grief, Junior! Everyone will know we've been sleeping together. He said so."

"And you said you love me."

She sighed in exasperation. "The cat's out of the bag."

"Yeah."

"Whoever gets you in the auction, you behave yourself, do you understand?" She instructed him. "I don't like the idea of what another woman could do to you. You're far too susceptible."

"Only to you. No other woman interests me."

"Promise you'll behave." She pushed for that. "At four dollars and fifty-one cents, I haven't a chance at winning you."

"And you only be civil to Tad."

"I keep trying to remember why I bid on him."

"You should have asked me first. You're really a pain, do you know that?"

"Let me up."

There were people all around them discussing what had happened. J.R. looked up, saw them and said, "Oh." As he tried to get up, he staggered and looked at his side where blood was dripping.

Jan screamed, "You were *shot!* Oh, Junior!" She moaned and fainted.

Ten

Jan came out of her faint as she was being put into an ambulance. She proved that she was similar to J.R. in that she immediately developed eight arms and legs, all of which were thrashing. People protested. She squeaked, "J.R. Is he dead?"

"No," said a strange voice. "Hold still. Cut that out!"

"I have to see him. Are you sure he's alive?"

"Damn it, J.R. Tell her to cut that out!"

"I'm fine," J.R.'s voice was weak.

In a pitiful voice, Jan begged to know: "Where did they shoot you? Are you going to live?"

"Probably."

A harsh voice cussed rather spectacularly and told J.R. to shove it.

Jan squirmed and wiggled and struggled. "Is he dying?"

"No!" shouted the nasty, impatient voice.

"Was it a police bullet?" She had to know.

"There were no shots! *It was your damned scissors!*" said the nasty voice.

She looked over at J.R. "Why is he so hyper?"

J.R. looked languishing. "Did you hear what wounded me?"

"My scissors."

"Doesn't it bother you a little that you rammed your scissors into me?"

With great tears rolling down her cheeks, her head wobbled in agreeing bobs. "I was going to do that to that bank robber. Where did I get you? It was your fault I did that, you jerked me so unexpectedly. And I had a death grip on the scissors."

"Right between my ribs. You missed my heart."

She wailed.

That nasty voice threatened, "J.R., you tell her the truth."

"I *said* she missed my heart."

The voice snarled, "J.R.!"

He sighed in irritation. "It's only a scratch."

"Oh, Junior, you're so brave."

He agreed.

The nasty voice said, "The only reason we're taking you in is that we want to be sure that sleaze doesn't have any buddies around. We've picked up the other two, now. We've been their shadows."

"You got them all?"

"This one was the only one missing. So we just watched the other two. If we'd pulled them in, the third guy might have taken off."

"J.R., are you okay?"

"Yeah, honey. You missed my—"

That nasty voice said something obscene.

J.R. scolded, "She knows what those words mean. You ought not say them in front of her. She taught them to me."

"Tell her you're only scratched. Do it now. She's going to pass out again."

"Look at my side, honey. See? It's only a scratch."

She asked in a faltering voice, "How deep is the cut?"

The nasty voice snarled, "One one-hundredth of an inch."

"Aww." Her voice wavered.

The nasty voice said, "That hardly broke the *skin* on his thick hide!"

"Then he'll live?"

And the nasty voice snarled, "Forever. Just watch. He's the type."

J.R. complained, "She was getting on such a great guilt trip. If you'd shut up, I would have had her in the palm of my hand. Peacock-feather fans and grapes dropped into my mouth—"

"Then—" her voice held a funeral note "—you'll be able to go to the auction tonight?"

"No problem," replied the snarler.

"Oh." Such a tiny sound.

"You don't want him to?"

"I only bid four dollars and fifty-one cents."

"That's 'way over his worth," the snarler assured her.

"Someone else might not know him as well as we do," she mentioned gloomily, her eyes very sad.

"It's like my wife says, 'There's no accounting for taste.'"

"You are discussing me, and I'm right here. That's rude."

The snarler said mildly, "At least we aren't bragging about you and embarrassing you."

"I snatched her out of there and she got me with her scissors. Do you realize the trauma I've been through in this almost last hour of my life?"

Snarler said, "You can handle it."

"Oh, J.R. You were magnificent."

"I was scared silly." His voice was again weakened.

She assured him, "No one knew."

"You've got to quit attracting other men."

She became indignant. "I have never tried."

"You bid on Tad."

She soothed, "That was my bid, not his."

"He picked up your papers in the school yard that time."

"He's just automatically polite."

"I got you out of the hall. I was the only one you would trust to do that and not fight."

"I trust you."

"I want you to love me."

The snarler watched and listened, turning his head from one to the other, fascinated. He felt as if he was in the middle of a poorly directed TV show with lousy dialogue and no station choice.

She was saying, "Oh, J.R...."

He put his hand to his side and groaned faintly.

Great tears leaked from her eyes.

The snarler was impressed. He went home that night, loomed over his little wife and took off his cap as he sighed gustily and said, "It's a jungle out there."

And she said, "I saw you got the third guy. They had a picture on the TV of you cuffing him. I taped it on the VCR. You looked great."

"All in a hard day's work."

"You have to fight off any of those women?"

"I didn't notice 'em."

"You look so dangerous in that uniform. Why don't you take it off?"

See? It was easy. And he knew he lived in really sharp writing with great direction, and when he retired from the force, he'd make his fortune writing for TV cop shows.

Jan and J.R. went back to the hall to find everyone a little stimulated and excitable in greeting them, but someone else had handily finished all the bouquets and they had even been placed on the tables. The two lovers stood around, not volunteering exactly, but no one asked them to do anything, so they went back to Jan's.

She cried. She bawled and shivered with delayed reaction, and he held her, saying, "It's okay."

She finally washed her face in cold water and shrieked when she looked into the mirror. He came rushing in, and she wailed, "Look, I'm all blotchy."

"You don't cry enough. You wait a couple of years in between times and then, when you do, it all comes at once. But a woman that's been threatened with abduction by a bank robber has reason to be upset."

"I was afraid that something would happen to you," she explained. "I've watched out for you all our lives, and that's what worried me so much when you were away from me. I wondered if you were managing alone."

He nodded. "That's why I had to leave you. I had to know I could be self-sufficient. You could make the most harebrained schemes sound logical. I had to get a better perspective on things so I could keep us whole."

With some censure, she put in: "I didn't know if the armwave was to go out the back door or lie down on the floor."

He managed to understand she was talking about the signal they'd given her when the bank robber was trying to get her to go with him. "If the hand had spread out and lowered toward the floor, that would have meant lie down. Waving once to the rear of the hall meant to leave, so that you would go past me and I'd get you out of there."

Stiffly she said, "I didn't know there were those nuances."

"You chose the right one."

"I have to see your side to be sure it's all right." She was agitated. "It looked like a gaping hole."

"I think it's already healed."

"Let me see."

"You want me out of my clothes," he guessed. "You're just looking for an excuse to get me out of my clothes."

"Let me see."

He smiled and unbuttoned his shirt and showed her the scratch. It was long and angry-looking, but it wasn't dangerous.

"I might have killed you."

"I don't kill easy. If I did, I would have died of fright when you convinced me we could walk that trestle I'd been *forbidden* to set foot on."

"I'd timed the trains."

"It was abandoning my parents' control and giving control to you."

"Do I control you?"

"I'm the guy running back and forth between houses, fetching what I need."

"What do you need?" she asked him solemnly, her eyes very large and her mouth soft.

"To be with you." His throat clacked in the silence.

"To make love."

He barely shook his head as he replied slowly, "Not all the time. But to be around you. You're magic to me."

"I love you, J.R."

"Yeah."

He picked her up and carried her upstairs to the rocking chair where he sat and held her, rocking her slowly. She could feel how much he wanted her, but he didn't mention it at all. He just held her and rocked her.

She asked softly, "How many kids are we going to have?"

He blinked a time or two, then he said, "We're only allowed two and one-third children."

"I always thought of the one-third as a much smaller child. Patsy thought it was one leg and half the body. She thought that wasn't very nice."

He explained, "That's because women don't really understand math."

"In the national math test in high school, *most* of the top third were women."

"That's only school work."

"Is this part of the Male Chauvinist red book?" she inquired in a rather stilted manner.

"Yeah. A book of hard facts."

"It occurs to me that the reason you have to wear a hard hat is that your brain is mush."

"You make it that way. I dream of you and think about you and want to be in you."

"Oh?"

"And if you don't quit wiggling your fanny around that way, you're going to find out how."

She sat very still, tilting her head sideways in quick little peeks, and he smiled wickedly.

He had his cordless phone, and it did ring. He was needed to evaluate the site. So he went out.

That night was the night of the Garden Club's auction.

Jan had to dress early and be down at the hall, so she went ahead when the time came. Therefore, J.R. didn't see Jan's purple dress on her until he arrived. He was sitting at their table talking to a guy, and she came over with some extra pink napkins, counting, seeing to it that there were enough. Because of the unexpected interest, and therefore the surge in ticket sales, they'd had to seat ten people at each table.

J.R. surprised Jan, in that he arrived in formal clothing. She'd only thought that he'd wear a suit. The men attending were about half in suits and half in tuxedos, but each of the men in the auction wore a tux, and so did J.R. He looked gorgeous.

She smiled at him as she leaned supplying a missing napkin to the table, and he gasped. But oddly enough, the thing he first noticed was that the smooth medallion was caught between her breasts so firmly that the chain hung in a curve from her chest, but the medallion stayed put. He looked at the guy with him and, sure enough, he was enjoying the view.

She went busily on to another table. J.R. excused himself and followed after her. She bustled off into the side hallway and he caught up with her there. He said, "I need another napkin."

"Oh? Okay." She got him one.

He shook it open, but then he reached and slowly pulled the medallion from between her breasts. She watched his face. The medallion came free, and he saw that it was a thin, flat blue stone. What...? Then he looked up at her eyes and saw they matched the color of the stone exactly.

He stared at her, and she blushed just a little. Then he remembered. Their church group had been up at the dunes on Lake Michigan. It must have been eight years ago, and in the wash of waves along the shore, he'd found some of the stones and given them to her. He'd said they matched her eyes. And she wore one. He was very moved.

She started to turn away, but he stopped her and growled, "If you lean over again, your lungs are going to fall out." He tucked the medallion carefully back into place, then he tied one side of the napkin around her throat, leaving the rest down over her décolletage.

She looked down at her covered chest, then up into J.R.'s waiting eyes. She recognized his covering her as a test. She could do anything, and it would only be an incident in their lives. It would change nothing. But her eyes held just the tiniest bit of a smile, and he saw that.

Again she turned away and went about her business. He went back to their table, but he saw her later. Her back was to him, and he watched. She turned around, and a jolt went through him as he saw that the napkin was still in place. His heart melted.

When she finally came and sat beside him, she was still wearing the napkin. Sadly she asked him, "Who do you think will win you?"

"You."

She scoffed. "At four dollars and fifty-one cents?"

"No one else can have me."

Dinner was served, and with the mob of people that took time. But the meal was okay, and the chatter in the hall was of high volume. There was a very nice festive air. There was laughter, and it was a gala.

Jan didn't laugh much. She was nervous and depressed. She could handle Tad. He was nice enough, but she sweat over who would win J.R. And she eyed the women throughout the hall, and knew they were all prettier, more clever and far more aggressive than she.

It took forever to clear the tables and serve dessert. And the time dragged. The noise volume was irritating to Jan. She wanted the evening to be finished.

She didn't want to win Tad.

As their names were called, each of the five men went up onto the platform, and people cheered and applauded. She thought Tad looked like a nice clotheshorse. She thought J.R. looked like every woman's dream. And that depressed her because she knew all the other women's stares were on J.R., and their eyes all glittered with lust for his body. She didn't have a chance.

Paul's name was first. He blushed and felt awkward, but Phyllis was just darling and so pleased her bid had won him that he was flattered.

So to be polite, Jan knew that she would *have* to smile and seem pleased when she won Tad. How was she going to smile?

Mickey was next, and he was a clown, anyway. He swaggered up to the platform and posed and acted hilariously. And Ginger won him and there was laughter and cheers. He had been such a smarty, but when he saw Ginger, he became quiet and avid. She was a little embarrassed by her blush of pleasure.

How was Jan ever to make it seem like fun for her to win Tad?

John was next. There were whoops and hollers over to one side of the hall and so obviously Connie's friends were excited for her.

Next was Tad, which surprised Jan. She'd thought he would be last. She got ready, trying to mask her lack of enthusiasm . . . and *Silthy* was called!

Jan was astonished, and almost faint with relief.

But then J.R. was still up there. He would be the last one claimed. Her dread filled her pores. Who would get J.R.? *And her name was called!* She had him? For four dollars and fifty-one cents! She laughed as she stood up. And cheers rang through the hall. Probably there wasn't any more noise than for the others, but it sounded roaring in her ears.

J.R. had a smug smile on his face and watched her coming up to the stage to claim him. She was wearing that purple dress and pink napkin. She was really something. He laughed in his delight of her.

She took his hand, her grin big and she said, "A bargain, at that price."

"What price?" he grinned at her.

"Four dollars and fifty-one cents."

"Yeah."

They turned grinning to the audience who laughed and cheered, since he was the last one auctioned. Jan raised her fist in triumph, and he raised their clasped hands.

Minna was there with her cameraman.

The five couples danced the first dance. J.R. wrapped his arms around Jan and shifted a little from one foot to the other, but he didn't move. She loved it. But the next three dances were for ladies who paid a dollar each to cut in on the men they'd bid on but lost.

Jan felt a little sorry for J.R. because her getting him at four dollars and fifty-one cents showed that no one else had bid on him. Other than the committee, who'd all bid one cent less than Jan.

But with the second dance, women lined up! And J.R. didn't stand there hugging, he danced! He smiled over women's shoulders at Jan and, along with his feet, his eyes danced. He'd fooled her. She would have been more amused by him, if it hadn't been for the long line of women.

Then she assumed that the bid trio had finally listened to her, and they'd switched the five hundred to J.R. The softies.

So she began asking along the line, "What did you bid on Junior?"

She got some idea of how foolish women can be to get a date. But one woman said, "Six hundred dollars. I really thought I had him."

Six hundred?

And Jan became thoughtful. How could she have won J.R. over a six-hundred-dollar bid? The bid trio weren't dishonest. They wouldn't have fixed the books. But obviously a mistake had been made. Jan wasn't going to ask for a recount and lose him. She decided the woman was lying. She probably hadn't even bid on J.R., and she was just flattering him.

That was kind of the women. But when Jan's turn came to dance with J.R., the biddy clung to him and rubbed against him, and there wasn't a thing he could do. His eyes sparkled and he glanced over at Jan and bit his lip so that he wouldn't laugh. He was enjoying himself.

After the fourth dance, the winning women were supposed to have their prizes to themselves. That didn't work in several instances. So Silthy took Tad out of there, and they weren't seen again. There were whispers and hushed-up laughter over that.

No one could get John's attention. And Mickey just wouldn't let go of Ginger. J.R. was besieged. At first he saw to it that Jan had a partner before he would dance with any of the women. But she did get to dance with him, and he did dance.

She leaned back in his arms and commented, "You can dance."

"Yeah."

"You didn't at the barn."

"I wanted so bad to hold you against me, and it seemed like a very easy way to do it without scaring hell out of you."

"You fooled me."

"A time or two." He shrugged and executed a perfect turn, then moved her out and back to him again. He made her look good because he knew how to lead and he knew how to signal her so that she knew what he was trying to do. There was more to dancing than knowing how to move the feet. She loved it.

And he said, "Sorry" to the women who tried to cut in. He said that to some men who wanted to dance with Jan. He danced with her. And she smiled. She was still wearing the napkin around her neck, and there were comments on that, but she just said, "J.R. doesn't like the top of my dress."

That led to some curiosity among the males who then wanted to judge the top of her dress for themselves. J.R. declined their petitions.

As they danced, Jan said, "I'm having a good time."

"Let's go to bed."

"I dreaded this night so much. I was so worried who'd get you. Some lecherous female who would suck you dry of blood with her pointed teeth."

"I was perfectly safe."

He seemed so secure. She would never tell him that the bid trio had rigged the books. Their reputations were safe with her. She smiled up at J.R. and said, "You're worth every penny of the four dollars and fifty-one cents."

"I know. Let's go to your place and go to bed. I want to examine that stone again."

"Take off the napkin. You can see it now. It's outside my dress."

"Why did you wear it inside, between those nice round breasts, and drive me crazy with curiosity?"

"I didn't want you to know I was pining for you." She gave him an uncomplicated look.

"Did you pine for me?"

She agreed: "For the longest time. I didn't know whom I would marry."

"So you bid on . . . Tad."

She shrugged. "He's innocuous. I wouldn't have had any trouble with him."

"If I hadn't shown up, you'd have married him for lack of something better to do. You'd have taken him in hand and changed the course of his life. He made a lucky escape. You'd have had him running for Congress."

She accepted that. "Probably. He'd be good at politics."

"You'd be too much for him. He wouldn't know how to handle you."

"But you do?"

He took a deep breath. "I've made a lifelong study of you, and I know exactly what to do about you under any circumstances. You are always getting yourself into binds of one kind or another, and I always have to get you out."

"If I tell you this, you are never to refer to it again. Do you understand?"

"Now what have you done?" He was forebearing.

"Remember that night when I pretended to go to sleep on your back steps?"

"Who could forget that night? I got you. Finally. That's the biggest thing that's ever happened to me."

"Me, too."

He grinned down at her. "What do you have to confess?"

"I was there to chide you about impropriety."

He burst out laughing. "That's why you tried to get away. Your conscience got to you? But I tracked you down and finally got you in the volunteer tomato plants."

"Don't ever refer to it again."

"Getting you?"

"The reason I was there," she clarified. "Since I seduced you so adroitly, I think it was funny that I did that on such a mission . . . being there to scold you for your conduct."

"You like my conduct."

"Very much." She gave him a secret little smile.

"Let's go home and go to bed. Let's be rash to-night, and try my bed."

"Uh, can I agree to that without seeming too un-ladylike and eager?"

"I love you, Buttercup."

"That's so nice to hear." She smiled tenderly. "Let's go."

His chuckle was wicked.

So they were really tangled up together in his bed when the police raided her house. The lovers peeked out of his upstairs windows and watched a Keystone Cops chase that was incredible. They looked at each other and asked, "What?"

When things quieted down a little and people had quit running, J.R. pulled on his trousers and went over to her house and inquired as to what the hell was going on?

"He got away, and we figured he'd come here. He did, and we got him again."

"The bank robber?"

"Yeah. Don't tell her. It would only scare her."

Then somebody asked, "Where is she?"

"With me."

As they looked up at his windows, they saw her duck out of sight. They clapped J.R. on the shoulder and said, "Good thing you were over there."

"Keep an eye on that guy, will you?"

"Don't worry. We've got him now."

So J.R. stood around outside in his bare chest and jeans until the last of the people and neighbors left. And Mrs. Witherspoon mentioned, "I'm glad you're taking good care of her, but how did you hear about the escape?"

"The grapevine." His face was earnest as he lied.

"Oh. Well, you were very smart to take her over to your house. I would have offered mine, if I had known, but I'm just as glad you took care of her. The excitement isn't good for Ralph."

"I'll handle her."

"Yes." Mrs. Witherspoon looked down his strong, young body and smiled. "I'll just bet you do."

It wasn't until a month later that the auction committee met and cleared away the nagging tail ends of the Mid-Summer Festival. They'd made almost six thousand dollars.

J.R.'s poster had sold surprisingly well, and a national distributor had picked it up. J.R. got a dollar for each poster sold. If it went well nationally, he could make a small fortune. So would the Garden Club.

And it was Minna who said privately to Jan, "It was J.R.'s thousand that put you over the top. Here's your check back."

"What?"

"He said he didn't want anyone else to win him, and he couldn't tolerate Tad having you for the weekend, so he was adding that to your bid. He swore us to secrecy. Since Silthy outbid you on Tad, we have to give you back your grandmother's money. You tried so hard to change your bid, and we love you. So although we know, and you know, you are sworn right now that you will never allow J.R. to know we told you about his increasing your bid. Promise?''

Jan hugged Minna. "I promise on my woman's oath.''

"That'll do fine.''

And she found time to discreetly hug Carol and say thanks to her and the same to Peggy. Both cautioned her that she must never, never, never tell J.R.. A woman *never* allowed a man to think she could break her word. It would be bad for the gender. Jan agreed.

So in the years to come, she would mention occasionally that J.R. was well worth every penny put into the bid. She called him her best bargain. And she said they would need to find a lot and plant some trees so that she could do her share, past the four dollars and fifty-one cents she'd contributed.

And he would smile.

When they made love and it was especially sweet and tender, she would say, "If I had just known how good you were, I would have bid a little more on you.''

Once as they lay replete and smiling, he questioned Jan: "Why were you in the bank the day of the robbery?''

She looked startled.

"You never told me." He slowly fished that slender blue oblong rock out from between her breasts. "What were you doing there?''

"I...was...seeing Phyllis about my debts.''

"Oh? Why did you have to do that on a rainy day?''

"You can get in quicker." She was glib. "Not many people go to banks in rainy weather.''

"Except for you and bank robbers.''

"Well...''

"So what about your debts?''

"They are all doing well."

"I can pay them off." He offered.

"No. Thanks, but I want you to start your business and—"

"What business is that? This?" And he put his hand on her.

"—so you'll be home more."

He was thoughtful. "You want me to start *that* business? Why do you want me home more?"

"I like having you around."

"It's a good thing."

But he took care of the business at hand, too. He bent her back onto the bed and kissed her nicely for a time while he captured her attention again. Then he did all the delicious things he knew so exactly pleased her. Then he teased and sampled her until she was avidly interested. And he allowed her to become bold with him. But he was very forward, so he took over and showed her how it was done, yet again.

He mentioned how patient he was in training her. She said it was he who was slow, but what could she expect, having won him with a bid of only four dollars and fifty-one cents?

He promised that he would try to live up to her great expectations.

And in all those long, good years together, she never, never, never told.

And neither did he.

*   *   *   *   *

Silhouette Special Edition

proudly presents
the long-awaited ''prequel'' volume of

★ **LOVE AND GLORY** ★

by
LINDSAY McKENNA

Dawn of Valor

In the summer of '89, Silhouette Special Edition premiered three novels celebrating America's men and women in uniform: LOVE AND GLORY, by bestselling author Lindsay McKenna. Featured were the proud Trayherns, a military family as bold and patriotic as the American flag—three siblings valiantly battling the threat of dishonor, determined to triumph . . . in love and glory.

Now, discover the roots of the Trayhern brand of courage, as parents Chase and Rachel relive their earliest heartstopping experiences of survival and indomitable love, in

Dawn of Valor, Silhouette Special Edition #649.

This February, experience the thrill of LOVE AND GLORY—from the very beginning!

DV-1

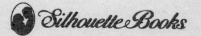

Silhouette Books

SILHOUETTE·INTIMATE·MOMENTS®

FEBRUARY
FROLICS!

This February, we've got a special treat in store for you: four terrific books written by four brand-new authors! From sunny California to North Dakota's frozen plains, they'll whisk you away to a world of romance and adventure.

Look for

L.A. HEAT (IM #369) by Rebecca Daniels
AN OFFICER AND A GENTLEMAN (IM #370) by Rachel Lee
HUNTER'S WAY (IM #371) by Justine Davis
DANGEROUS BARGAIN (IM #372) by Kathryn Stewart

They're all part of February Frolics, coming to you from Silhouette Intimate Moments—where life is exciting and dreams do come true.

FF-1

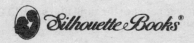

Silhouette Books®

Take 4 bestselling love stories FREE

Plus get a FREE surprise gift!

Silhouette romances are now available in stores at these convenient times each month.

Silhouette Desire
Silhouette Romance

These two series will be in stores on the 4th of every month.

Silhouette Intimate Moments
Silhouette Special Edition

New titles for these series will be in stores on the 16th of every month.

We hope this new schedule is convenient for you. With only two trips each month to your local bookseller, you will always be sure not to miss any of your favorite authors!

Happy reading!

Please note there may be slight variations in on-sale dates in your area due to differences in shipping and handling.

SDATES

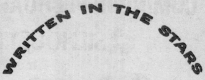
WRITTEN IN THE STARS

**Star-crossed lovers?
Or a match made in heaven?**

Why are some heroes strong and silent . . . and others charming and cheerful? The answer is WRITTEN IN THE STARS!

Coming each month in 1991, Silhouette Romance presents you with a special love story written by one of your favorite authors—highlighting the hero's astrological sign! From January's sensible Capricorn to December's disarming Sagittarius, you'll meet a dozen dazzling and distinct heroes.

Twelve heavenly heroes . . . twelve wonderful Silhouette Romances destined to delight you. Look for one WRITTEN IN THE STARS title every month throughout 1991—only from Silhouette Romance.

STAR

Silhouette Books®